Chasing

the

Milky

Way

erin e. moulton

SCHOLASTIC INC.

ISBN 978-0-545-83202-1

12 11 10 9 8 7 6 5 4 3 2 1   15 16 17 18 19 20/0

Printed in the U.S.A.   40

First Scholastic printing, February 2015

Edited by Jill Santopolo
Design by Semadar Megged
Text set in Imprint MT Std

For Ma
who acknowledges the humanity in us all

I have been one acquainted with the night.

—Robert Frost

One

SUNNYSIDE TRAILER PARK HAS EXACTLY one rooster. It belongs to Mr. Blinks and his name is Chuck. Mr. Blinks sold the whole coop and this one, too, but Chuck found his way right back to Sunnyside. That's typical. Once you're in Sunnyside Trailer Park, it's hard to leave, and it's not because of the good cooking or family-friendly folks. It's because it's a black hole of a place. The gravitational pull is so strong you never get out. At least not in one piece. That's what I'm thinking about as soon as Chuck starts bawling at 4:30 a.m. That's what I think about at this time every morning. Getting out of Sunnyside.

I make myself sit up, push my blankets down. The house still smells like old tomato soup. Last night's dinner. I stretch my legs and put my feet on the floor, glance out the window. Darkness is draping over the world like a big ratty blanket. Tiny holes strung up in the shape of constellations. I feel around for my flashlight. My little sister, Izzy, flips over in the bed next to mine. The springs squeak under her slight weight.

"Time, Lucy?" Izzy says.

"Not yet," I whisper. I pull a pair of jeans up off the floor and throw them on. "Just Mission Control time."

I lean over and give her a kiss on her forehead.

"Me too?" she says.

"Nah, you sleep. We can play after school." I flick the flashlight on and jump out my window onto the ground. I walk over to the carport and pull back the tarp. The early morning dew makes the tarp cool and damp on my fingertips. I slide inside, tuck myself up along the junked-up Mustang and over to my Mission Control station. It's not much to look at. Just a run-down desk that Mr. Blinks got at work. He works at the junkyard, so he finds all sorts of great stuff.

I stifle a yawn and sit down at the desk. I pick up Walkie One and put it to my mouth. Press the speak button with my index and middle fingers.

"Mighty Hawk, this is Juniper Ray, captain of Vintage Carrier twenty-five twenty-five. You out there? Over," I say, letting my fingers off the button. I put the walkie up to my ear and listen. From outside, Chuck gives another wake-up call. I hear a clatter as Mr. Blinks hurls something out his window, but nothing comes in through Walkie One. I reach over for a pencil, wondering what is taking Cam so long. Then, just as I'm about to give up and carry on solo, the walkie crackles to life.

"Juniper Ray, this is Mighty Hawk. On my way. Over." The walkie goes silent, then comes back to life. "Did you get that joke? On my way. Over?" he says.

I slide the walkie from ear to mouth. "Hilarious, Cam."

His voice crackles through. "See you" *shhh* "in a few" *shhh* "over."

I place the walkie back in its spot and pick up our notebook, pulling it across the desk. The carport lights up with a green tint as I switch the desk lamp on. I press my fingers to either side of my watch so it flips from the current time to countdown. I've had a timer set for the past month. T-minus thirty-six hours from liftoff and T-minus seventy-five hours until competition. I glance to the corner of my desk where there is a picture of Gram staring out at me.

It's been a year since she went on an infinite voyage, jumped ship to another world. I give the picture a half-hearted wink and hug her memory close to me. I have promises to keep.

My fingers find the edge of my Mission Control notebook. I open it and scan the page for the one-hundredth time.

BotBlock Jr. Robot Challenge
June 15th 2013
15 Ocean Avenue
Seahook, NH

Categories:
Humanoid
*Junkbot
Tri-Bot

Mindstorm
Autonomous

Events:
Skills Test
BotBall
Dune Driving
Maze Runners (remote control)
Rescue Robotics
Unique Attributes

My gaze lands on the final line. The most important one:

Round Robin Winner Receives
$5,000 and 15% of college tuition

Me, Mama, Gram, and Izzy went to the seacoast every year since I was eight, not counting last year, due to tragedy. This year we're going, and this year is going to be different. One, because Gram isn't coming with us, not literally. Two, because this year I intend to compete in the robot competition. We usually just watch it because I've never been old enough, and the registration is expensive. "No how, no way, no money," I hear Mama's voice ringing in my ears. But you have to put some money in to get something out. This year Cam's coming along, too. We're skipping out on a day of school and going to the coast to win some prize money. We have to. We have to because no one needs it like we do.

I turn the page to our Mission Control Protocol for Optimum Achievement. It's gone through some revision.

~~Make money~~

~~Find our dads and start new life~~

1) Save up registration money
2) Complete, practice, and program PingPing200
3) Go to BotBlock Challenge (and win)
4) Make dreams come true (see dream charts, pages 7 and 8)

The plan for taking control of our lives is in place. . . . The only problem is we still haven't crossed off number one on our list, *Save up registration money*. Or number two on our list, *Complete, practice, and program PingPing200*. And three and four can't get done until the other two are done. But we'll figure it out. Cam and I have been saving up the money for registration since last year. And we almost have enough. We mowed lawns, raked leaves, and even accepted some charity.

I glance down at our robot. "We'll get it done. Right, PingPing?"

He stares straight ahead with his LED eyes, but I know he's on my side. "Somehow," I add. I swivel to have a better look at him. He's genuine junk. I mean it in the best way. All of his parts are from the junkyard. It started with a broken remote-control pickup truck. We tore off the sides, so that just the wheel and truck bed base were left, then attached a big body made from a Cheese Balls barrel. Cam found a deflated football and sliced it in half, so Ping-Ping has a genuine pigskin head. We poked two holes in it and ran power to two LED lights that serve as eyes. Of course, we had to rig up a new battery, a motor, a receiver, and a brain. You can see all his wiring right in his stomach. He looks like a trashy R2-D2, but I like to believe he has the same type of noble heart. We completed his arms last week, but we've still got a ways to go.

I flip the battery on. His eyes send bright beams toward the back of the carport. *Wuw-whir, wuw-whir.* His claws and elbows jolt as he fires to life. I hear the tarp crinkle and look over my shoulder. Cam walks in and falls back, shielding his face with his arm. I turn PingPing to the side so it's not a direct hit.

Cam stumbles away from the light, around the other side of the Mustang.

"You escaped?" I ask.

"Good one!" he says, coming over to the Mission Control station. The truth is, Cam doesn't have to sneak. His mom doesn't have a clue where he is, and doesn't care either. Cam is one of what my ma calls "Mrs. McKinney's seven feral children." They range from four months to twelve years and white to black. Cam's the oldest and the blackest. He's also my best pal.

"Mighty Hawk at your service, Cap'n." He pulls a crate over and sits on it. His white T-shirt glows in the stark light. I unhook the remote control from its spot around PingPing's neck and put the lanyard around my own. I flip it on.

"We have a ton to do." We've come a long way, but we still need to practice for the remote control maze run. We need to finish his program for the rescue mission. And, if Mr. Blinks comes through, we need to attach a metal detector for the "unique attributes" part of the competition. I toggle to the right and inch to the left, then hit the joystick forward. PingPing speeds along the side of the Mustang. I slide over the door and into the driver's seat so I can see all around the car to maneuver him.

"Hey, Juniper Ray, you wanna stop for a minute?" Cam jumps up next to me in the car.

"Do I really need to remind you that we're running way behind on our Protocol for Optimum Achievement?" I say.

"It'll just take a second. I got you something." I let up and PingPing halts at the passenger-side door. I lean against the seat and look at Cam. He pulls a rectangular block from his pocket. Flips it over. *Hershey's,* it says.

I let go of the remote control and let it hang around my neck. My mouth starts watering. "Cam, you shouldn't have bou—"

"Who said I bought it! I said I GOT you something." A smirk plays across his face.

"You stole it?" I whisper, taking the bar from his hand.

"Not from the store. Just from someone who didn't deserve it!" he says.

He must have taken it from his mom's current boyfriend, Dwayne. We pronounce it D-Wayne. D standing for dimwit, doofus, dumb as a doornail.

"Well, what's done is done." I pull a fold until the wrapper drops onto the ground, break a small corner off and hand it to Cam. He throws it up into the air and catches it in his mouth. It clicks on his teeth as it lands. I break another piece and pop it into my mouth.

"Thanks, Mighty Hawk," I say, letting the chocolate melt on my tongue. He scarfs his down pretty fast and I hand him another, bigger piece. I chew fast, too, so I can get back to PingPing.

When the whole bar is gone, I crumple up both of the wrappers and shove them into my pocket.

"Happy birthday," Cam says.

"Thanks," I say as I pick the RC back up.

"Wait! I almost forgot." Cam digs into his other pocket.

"I'm all ears," I say, but I press my thumb forward and send PingPing racing around the front of the car.

"This wasn't stolen. It was won fair and square." Cam holds his hand up. A dollar is hanging from his fingers. I stop PingPing again.

"Mission Control fun," Cam says.

"*Fund*," I say. "Anyway, where'd you get this one? You should give it to your mom or something." Of course I don't want Cam to give Mission Control money to his mom, but I know she could use it. Just yesterday I saw the four-year-old, Mickey, eating a clover on the back step. I don't know if it was because of the lack of other options or if she just likes the taste, but still.

Cam tilts his head. "Really? You think I'm gonna give this to Professor Evil?"

He grabs my left hand and presses the dollar bill into it. "It's ours," he says. Then he cartwheels onto the floor. He doesn't nail the landing; instead he fumbles and rolls into a bucket, which topples over, sending tools everywhere. He lands crumpled in the too-narrow space between the car and the house.

"Not your best move," I tell him.

"You think?" he says as he stands. He dusts off his blue jeans and lifts the tarp up. "I can't stay 'cause Brian was up already and not feeling good. I'll see you in an hour. And I promise I'll help after school. Happy birthday!"

I nod. Something is always coming up.

"Thanks." I fold the dollar bill and tuck it into my pocket. Cam ducks out.

"Hey, wait!" I shout. The tarp shuffles and he reappears. "Don't forget to pack. We leave tomorrow night. And we're not going late."

"Got it!" he says, letting the tarp drop.

I steer PingPing around the corner to where the mess of tools is still scattered across the path. "You think we can make it, buddy?" I speed him toward the mess, hard right, soft left, around a wrench, then hard right and straight to the wall, then soft left to a bin. Pretty soon he's past the tools and heading toward the back of the carport and around the car again.

"Lucy?"

PingPing and I both stop and look toward the trailer.

"Lucy, where are you?" It's Mama.

I dig into my pocket and pull the dollar bill out. Then I flip the remote control off and jump out of the Mustang.

"I'll be right there!" I shout. I kick over an upside-down milk crate and pull a paint can from beneath it. Mission Control fund. I feel for the screwdriver in the corner, then jam it underneath the lid and pry until the lid pops off, revealing our money stash. I check over my shoulder, making sure no one's around. I pull out the wad, add the bill. Then I take a little scrap of paper and pencil from the can. I cross out *351.50* and write *352.50*. Still short seven fifty. I would ask Mama for the remainder, but the whole reason the registration is a big secret is because money is nowhere to be seen around here.

"Lucy?" Mama says again. I jump, trying to pinpoint where her voice is coming from. A strawberry-flavored breeze wafts my way and my heart rises into my throat. Could it be birthday cupcakes? I push the money into the paint can, grab a hammer, and tap along the outer edge. I flip the milk crate over it and secure the hiding spot. I make my way back around to PingPing, flip him off, and slide him under the work station.

"You'll have to wait. As usual," I say.

The sides of his football head seem to tilt down the teensiest little bit. "You just gotta believe in the mission. We'll finish you up. I promise." The last bit is more to Gram's picture than to my robot. I blow a faraway kiss to the great beyond, then flick the light off and head inside.

Two

As I climb in the window and bounce off my bed, I smell that strawberry cake batter, but there's something burn-y about it, too. I sniff and head into the living room.

And stop.

It doesn't look like it did last night. When we went to bed it was all clean. Mama's desk had a few open books on it, but otherwise everything was mostly in order. I scan the room. Now the books are . . . everywhere. Some lie open, some closed, some are hugging on to others like their covers are arms. Some lie flat like they flew off the shelves with open wings. I can't even see the coffee table. It's got books, magazines, and newspapers. There's a shoe jammed in the bookshelf and a book in the shoe bin. The dehydrator that Mama uses about once a year is in the middle of the floor and it's got a bunch of dandelions in it.

"Mama?" I say, heading toward the kitchen. When I swing the door open, the smoke billows toward me and I cover my nose and mouth with my hand, blink my eyes. The kitchen looks like a bomb exploded in it and the smoky-sweet smell is strong. Mama has finished the cupcakes. Yup, they're done all right. A tinful sits on the stovetop, looking more like charred barbecue chickens than birthday-morning treats. Mama is nowhere to be seen. I open the door leading back into the living room and crane my neck. "Mama?" I put my ear up to listen, but if she's anywhere in here, she doesn't want to be found. Why'd she call me in the first place?

I go over to the table. It's like everything in Mama's head fell out her ears. Mama's a writer. She used to be a professor at Columbia University in New York City, but story has it that when I came along she thought it would be best to raise kids in the country, so she moved back to Vermont so we could be close to Gram. She worked at Bennington for a while. Then things got hard. So hard that we ended up in Sunnyside.

I push aside a few crumpled pieces of paper. Lift a book and look at the board above the table. There are articles pinned to it. Articles about the Curiosity Rover. *Tell Lucy* is scribbled in the margin. Next to it is an article headlined ROBERT FROST SCENIC BYWAY, and to the right there's something about the FBI. Pinned underneath is a list titled "Seahook":

Seahook

Go to Science and Nature Center
Eat at the Lobster Pound
Walk on the beach
Eat shaved ice

Watch the BotBlock Challenge
Midnight wishes
DON'T FORGET TO PACK

There are also a few poems and doodles pinned up. I look down at the table. A cluster of papers and envelopes are spread out next to each other, like they're supposed to fold and seal themselves. I spot the stem of a tipped-over wineglass. I reach out and grab it. Pull it up and turn it. A little drop in the bottom of the glass spins and smears across the side.

I eye the number for Dr. Vincent tacked to the board next to the door. When Gram passed away, Mama seemed like she wanted to follow her, at least halfway. Mama's right foot is still planted next to Izzy and me here in Sunnyside Trailer Park, but her other foot is behind Gram, trying to journey into a world we can't see. I don't blame her for missing Gram. I'd run out behind her, too, if I could.

"Hey, Mama!" I shout. I put the glass in the sink. This is the one spot in the house that looks cleaner than the rest. That's funny 'cause last night it was the only place in the house that was a mess. I open the cupboard. No plates? Just as I close the door, I spot Mama through the window. She's got the dish bin. And a shovel. I check the other houses and pray it's still early enough that no one will be around to witness this. I hurry out the door and around the side of the trailer. Mama's wearing a kerchief over her curly hair, big sunglasses, and a jacket. She's breathing heavy as she digs into the dirt.

"Morning, Mama," I say, taking it easy, stepping over to her like I'm walking on glass.

"If I have to look at one more goddamned dish," Mama says, putting one of the teacups into the ground. She covers it with dirt and moves a foot to the right and starts digging again. I see three little mounds running alongside the trailer. Three tiny gold-edged handles barely peeking out of the freshly dug soil. Like she's trying to grow a new set of china. I hear some roots pop free as she pulls up another layer of ground, dumping it to the side.

"Constant goddamned mess," Mama says.

"Isn't that more work than washing them?" I say, putting my hands into my pockets, trying to act casual.

Mama laughs, tilting her head back to the sky. "It's not the washing. It's the look of them. If I have to look at one more flower on one more china teacup I'm going to lose it. Absolutely lose it."

"You take your meds today?" I ask, thinking she is kind of already losing it. She freezes. Then starts shaking her head.

"Lucille, I'll remind you that I'm the parent. I'm the adult."

The light in Mrs. Barlow's trailer flicks on. She's the eyes and ears of the whole park, and I don't really feel like being part of her morning broadcast. Not today. I pick up the bucket of dishes. "I can wash these and put them in the cupboard, okay? Then you don't have to look at them. They'll be in the cupboard. Okay?"

Mama stops and looks from side to side, then she reaches into the pocket of her oversized jacket and pulls out a book, *The Poetry of Robert Frost*. Mama is stuck on Robert Frost 'cause she is a Robert Frost scholar. Meaning she has talked a lot about him and read a lot about him and even written some articles about him. She runs her finger along the index, tears out a page, and puts it into her pocket. She drops the rest of the book into the freshly dug soil and covers it quickly.

"You're right. We'd better get inside." She stomps on the fresh mound and then heads around the house to the door of the trailer, pulling the poem from her pocket and rubbing it between her fingers. We walk inside.

"Mama, maybe you should call Dr. Vincent," I say as I set the dish bin in the sink.

But she swats my words right out of the air. "No, no, I don't think so. He won't want to hear from me. I don't think so."

I flip the water on as Mama takes her glasses off her face. She closes her eyes, but I see them flick around underneath her lids, like she's searching for something in there. I wonder if she'll see my birthday.

"Are these cupcakes for me?" I say.

Mama opens her eyes. "Who do you think they're for?" she asks.

I flip the light above the sink on and Mama slaps her hand over her face.

"Way too bright," Mama says. "Too goddamned bright. How can I get any work done? Much less pack for vacation. It's impossible to move." She puts her sunglasses back on and settles into a chair at the table.

I flip the light off, grab the dish soap, and shake the last bit out of it. I look at Mama out of the corner of my eye. "I can help you pack after school if you don't get it done by then. I don't mind."

She gives off an exasperated groan. "I'm sure I can pack my own bag, Lucille." She slumps in her chair. I don't press it 'cause I can see she's blasting off. That's what Gram would say if she were here. The first time this happened we were out on Route 36.

My seventh birthday. Mama was going to bring us to the carnival. But instead, halfway there she got an idea in her head that it would be more fun to bring a carnival to us. Two seconds later, she pulled into Best Buy and bought two cell phones.

"One for home and one for the road," she said.

Seconds after that, she had activated an account and was hiring the Ringling Circus to come and do a demonstration at Sunnyside Trailer Park. It was called Circus School. She filled out the paperwork online and a few keystrokes later she had deposited a whole bunch of money into it, and we were ready to be entertained. I couldn't believe it. The Peeveys, getting lions, tigers, and bears to roam around the trailers? Mama had a flare for making magic happen. Of course, I still had that carnival flyer in my hands. The rides looked awful tempting and it was going to take a while for the circus to get to Sunnyside. One thing I knew was that if you whine a tiny bit, adults get sick of it and do what you want. So I did. But this time, Mama got mad. She said we were ungrateful little brats. Yep, my own mother. She said that. Only it was like it wasn't her.

After she told me a thing or two about myself, she sped down the highway to the Camden General Store. Then she got out of the car and leaped into the bed of a pickup truck that was pulling out of the parking lot. And I sat glued to my seat, wondering what she was doing as she sped down the highway, far away from us.

We waited in the car for an hour. My eyes didn't leave that spot where the truck disappeared until a big scary trucker knocked on the window. I hunched way down and snuck closer to Izzy in case this guy was some psycho killer. He told us he wouldn't hurt us, but what type of psycho killer says, "Hey, open your door, I'm going to kill you." So we just buttoned up and stayed where we were. I wished right then I knew how to drive that car.

Luckily, a few seconds later something jingle jangled, and when I leaned up to see what the noise was about, I spotted one of Mama's new phones sitting right there on the seat. I called up Gram and she came and got us.

We got back to Sunnyside and Gram wrapped us in blankets and she called everyone in the phone book to see if they had seen my lost mama. No one had. No one did, not for a few days.

The second night without Mama I got to thinking we must have really upset her, to make her run away like that. I tried to keep my crying small so it wouldn't wake anyone up, but Gram sure had good ears for an old lady. She came into my room and sat down on the side of the bed.

"You have nothing to do with why your mama left," she said. Then she leaned up against the wall. "Lucy, you're old enough to know this now, so I'm going to tell you. I won't be around forever. I want you to be prepared for what's to come."

I sat up on my pillow and peered over to make sure that Izzy was genuine sleeping, not just faking it. Her thumb was hanging half out of her mouth and her breathing was long, so I nodded at Gram.

"Your mother has manic-depressive disorder."

"Manic what?" I said. Wondering if manic was the same as maniac. There was a kid in my class at Poughkeepsie that Mrs. Sophia called a maniac. He mostly jumped around a lot. It didn't seem the same as what Mama was doing.

Gram adjusted my blanket around my belly. "It's when—" She stopped and smoothed the corner of the sheet that was sticking out. "It's when you go three steps past imagination." I looked at her, wondering what the heck that was supposed to mean.

She leaned toward the window a little and looked up at the sky. One thing about the Peevey family is that everyone likes the look of the stars. She got a little glint in her eye. "It's like when one second you're so high you can taste the sweetness of the Milky Way."

I looked out the window, too, and pictured my head way up, blasting off past the clouds into deep space. Clear as crystal. Sweet as candy.

"That's good then," I said, thinking how happy you would be like that.

"It's better than good. It's sharp, it's quick. It's filled with purpose. But only for the moment. When you have manic-depressive disorder, the next second it's like you have your head in the sand, and any sort of critter can go wandering in one ear and out the other."

I slammed my mouth shut, thinking about plummeting in my spacecraft, crash-landing, and the suffocation of sand all around my head.

"When you're that far down, everything in your head gets all muddled up and confused. And sad."

I just looked at her, thinking of what that would be like. To have any manner of stuff running around inside your head, making you fuzzy and sad.

"Your mother has a mental illness," she said.

And just like that all of the sand and insects that I imagined running around in my head thundered down into my stomach and started churning. She kept talking about it, but it seemed like she switched into a different language all of a sudden. She said schizoaffectivesomething psychoticsomething episodes. Bipolar type. Mixed diagnoses. She must have seen *the look on my face as I tried to understand what the heck she was talking about, because she took a deep breath and put her hands on either side of my head.*

"I have a mental illness, too," she said. "It runs in the family. It takes a long time to understand."

Gram's eyes were filling up with tears. I put my hands on either side of her gray head, just like she was putting her hands on mine, and looked at her close. Her brain didn't seem very sick to me. Not as far as I could tell. Gram was the best and I started wondering if maybe mental illness was a good thing? I wondered other things, too. Could I catch it? Like a cold?

"Do I have a mental illness?" I whispered, wondering what an ill brain would feel like, wondering if I'd be able to detect mine coming down with something.

She pulled a Kleenex out of her pocket and wiped her nose. "You're not showing a predisposition to bipolarity, Lucy, not yet. And anyway, doctors, scientists, they're all on the case. They have medication that helps." Her teeth hit together as she said medication. I pictured little pills being crushed between her molars. "And there are other things you can do, too. To help balance the brain."

That night I went to sleep. The next day, they located Mama and she went to Kensington. We went and saw her there, played board games and stuff. But she didn't like it. Not one bit.

"Are those birthday cupcakes?"

I start so badly that I drop one of the dishes in the sink.

It splashes a lukewarm wave of water onto my stomach and legs. It's Izzy. Mama grumbles as she goes into the living room. I grab the towel from the handle on the oven and press it against my soaking pants.

"Smoky," Izzy says, coming over to the counter. She taps the cupcake closest to her.

"Yeah. They cooked a little too long." I throw the towel on the counter. "Let's get ready for school."

We go to our room. I change and get Izzy into a pair of semi-clean clothes.

"Backpack," I say, lifting it up. She adjusts it on her shoulders. I grab mine and we head toward the front door. As we pass through the living room, I see Mama lying on the couch, hugging a pillow. It's funny to be jealous of a pillow. But for just a second I am. For just a second, I want Mama to wrap me in her arms and say, "Happy birthday, baby girl. I love you." But I can see that that's not going to happen, not right now.

In the kitchen, I sift through the piles on the table, finding Mama's seven-day pill container underneath the papers. I shake it. The pills rattle, so I know she has plenty. I set it in the clear spot right in front of her stuff, so maybe she'll see it and get it into her head to take them.

"Ready?" Izzy grasps my hand.

"Ready," I say, as I pull the door closed.

"Hey, Lucy?" Izzy skips down the steps and I notice her ponytail is already working its way around to the side of her head.

"Yeah? Hold up." I grab it and pull it to the top, then tighten it.

"Happy birthday, anyway," she says.

I give her shoulders a squeeze. "Thanks."

But to be honest, it's not my birthday I'm worrying about. It's T-minus thirty-five hours until liftoff and seventy-four hours to competition. I wonder if Mama is going to be good enough to go. Without Gram we have no backup plan. We're piloting our own ship.

Three

"On your marks."

I lean forward and turn the pencil one more time, setting the canister on the floor.

"Get set!" Mrs. Shareze stands at the opposite end of the classroom, holding her clipboard, as we line the other side with our bottle-bottom racers.

"GO!" She throws a tissue into the air. I let go of the can. The pencil and the torque of the rubber band inside send it flying across the floor.

"Go go go!" Cam shouts as our racer bumps a can to the right. It spins off the track and ours takes the lead. A second later our racer peels across the finish line and the end-of-day bell rings at the exact same time.

"Cam and Lucy win!" Mrs. Shareze shouts, her voice a little hoarse from a cold, and the rest of the kids groan. Some groan because they didn't win and some groan because it is us that won. Cam grabs hold of the counter and does a back kick in celebration, and Mrs. Shareze's face goes from smiling to pinched and crumpled.

"Feet on the ground, Mr. McKinney!" she says, then in the same breath, "Everyone please collect your belongings, place your desks back into position in the middle of the floor, and line up for buses."

I go up to the front of the room to grab our racer.

"Can I borrow a laptop again tonight?" I ask, picking the can up off the floor.

"Yes you may. How's your robot coming?" she says as she walks over to her desk and puts her clipboard down on it.

"We're a little behind on programming, but he looks pretty sharp!" I tell her. I can't wait to show PingPing to Mrs. Shareze. She runs our robot club at school and I think she's going to be really impressed with what we've been able to do without any kits. I put the bottle-bottom racer on my desk and then push it across the floor to its spot next to Cam's desk.

Feet stampede past me as kids line up at the door. I pull out my backpack and put the laptop inside.

"Can we go?" Destin Hoffsteader asks from the front of the line.

"Yes. Go ahead," Mrs. Shareze says, clasping her hands. She turns back to me. "Lucy, will you stay behind for a minute?"

Destin sticks his tongue out at me as he pushes the door open, and my classmates spill out into the hallway. Cam stands around in the back of the room, his hands tucked into his pockets. But I can see staying still is taking a lot of concentration.

"I'll meet you at Mission Control," I say. He nods and ducks out the door. I turn to see Mrs. Shareze going over to her desk. She coughs into her elbow just like it shows on a poster in our classroom. It's supposed to stop the germs from spreading on everything, like door handles and countertops and computers. I'm thinking I appreciate that because I don't want to be getting sick for BotBlock. She rummages around in the top drawer and I wonder what she keeps in there. If it's good or bad or what.

"Listen if Destin said I did somethi—" I start, but then stop as Mrs. Shareze holds out her hand. A cream-colored envelope dangles from her fingertips.

"Happy birthday to my star student," she says.

My stomach shakes and I take a deep breath. "For me?" I take the card in my hand.

"I can't forget my most involved student's birthday." She winks and heads to the hook on the wall. She pulls her bag off the hook and puts it over her shoulder. I hold the envelope between my fingers. A birthday card. She heads for the door and grabs a few Kleenexes from the back counter. She sneezes into one as she steps out into the hallway.

"Thank you," I shout as the door begins to shut. I swing my bag to my shoulder and hurry after her. "Thank you!"

She turns and smiles. A second later I bust out of the school and into the sunny afternoon.

As I take a shortcut up Fielders Lane I think that this day is really looking up. I eye the big yellow sun through the early summer leaves. I'm going to stop in my favorite spot in the park and read the card that Mrs. Shareze gave me *for my birthday.*

I jog past the gates of Sickle Park and drop my bag between the big roots of a maple tree. I sit up against it and watch the sunlight land in soft puddles around me. A few helicopter pods spin like confetti to the ground. I run my finger under the seal of the envelope. I tear it just a teensy bit, by accident, and pull out the card. The front is bright yellow and says *Happy Birthday*. Before I even flip the card open, a picture falls out. It's a picture of someone in a space suit. Sally Ride. I recognize her immediately.

Mrs. Shareze knows how much I love Sally Ride. I stare out past the maple and birch trees at the pond in the distance. With a name like Ride it seems like you'd be thinking about movement all the time. Not like my name. Lucille Peevey. It has the word *pee* in it.

I look up at the treetops shifting and moving in the wind, and I imagine my new name. Something amazing. Something really great like Lucille Anna NASA. Lucille Anna Engineer. Lucille Anna Scientist. That's what my name should be.

Before I do anything else, I pull my ratty school binder out and push the picture of Sally Ride into the front cover, so she's staring out at me. I put it back into my backpack safe and sound, then I pick the card up and flip it open.

Dear Lucille,
Albert Einstein once said
"Imagination is more important than knowledge. For knowledge is limited to all we know and understand, while

imagination embraces the entire world, and all there ever will be to know and understand."

That quote reminds me of you. Keep thinking. Keep dreaming. Keep imagining and looking for answers in your new year. Shoot for the stars.

Happy Happy 12!

Best Wishes,
Mrs. Shareze

I hold the card to my heart and close my eyes, feeling that warm sun on my face. *Shoot for the stars.* My brain starts making a video behind my eyes. Cam and I are standing on a stage with our hands in the air. PingPing200 is between us. All the news reporters are pushing their way to the front of a cheering crowd to get our speeches and autographs. We're champions and every single person knows it.

What will you do next? they'll ask.

What colleges will you be attending? they'll want to know.

Thank you, baby girl, you fixed everything, Mama will say.

"Oh look! It's Looney Lucy."

My world crashes in and I blink my eyes open, recognizing the voice as the card gets taken out of my hands. It's Destin. He has two boys with him, who stand a little farther back and look at me like I might jump at them. I lean into the maple and scramble to my feet.

"You give me that back right now," I say, coming up to his level. I reach for the card.

"What are you going to do about it, trailer trash?" he says as he pushes his hand into my face. One of his fingers slides into my mouth, against my gums, and I twist my head to get away. The back of my head hits the tree and smarts, but I use it to my advantage and brace myself against it, lift both feet, and kick. He flails backward and trips over a tree root as I wipe at my mouth, trying to get the salty, sweaty palm-taste of Destin Hoffsteader out.

His buddies go to help him up and he drops the card. I dive for it, but the breeze seems to be on his side. It picks it up and spins it downhill. I grab my backpack and head after it. But it rolls farther. Faster.

"You stupid idiot. You tore my pants!" Destin shouts after me.

I don't respond, keeping my eye on that card turning and turning down the hill toward the duck pond. *Please no, please don't go for a swim.* I race after it, but it seems like that card doesn't want to be caught. It runs ahead of me. I reach the edge and stop. Just as I do, I hear Destin, breathing heavily, coming up behind me.

"Hope you know how to swim, Looney." I feel his foot hit the back of my knee.

I scramble for something to hold on to, but the only thing my hand can reach is the edge of that card. I close it in my fingers and fall like a bag of bricks into the pond. I feel my bag swing and pull hard against my neck. Like an anchor, it takes me down. Cold water invades my shirt, my jeans. My clothes billow out. I push my arms down, trying to control the rush of water. It's everywhere. I hit the muddy floor and push up, breaking through the surface. I gulp for air and try to clear my eyes to see if Destin is coming after me. But he's not. He stands on the bank clapping his hands.

"Get lost," I sputter, but it doesn't sound very bold with all the water coming out. There's mud on my arms. There's mud in my shirt. I pull a reed off my sleeve. I try to blink my eyes clear.

"Gladly," he says, and walks up the hill like he's marching up to a podium. He slaps hands with the two boys standing at the top. I wonder what I ever did to them.

I step through the mucky water toward the edge of the pond. Slow and sliding more than I'd like. As I rise, I loosen my fingers. The card in my hand is soaked and bent. My bag makes a loud *schwakk* sound and seems to release a bucket of water into the pond behind me.

Then I remember the laptop.

Mrs. Shareze is going to kill me. Worse. I won't be able to program PingPing tonight. Not if the laptop is destroyed. I swing the bag to my right shoulder and hug it to my chest, squeezing the last of the water out of it. *Please don't be ruined*, I think. *Please, please. Don't be ruined.*

Four

THERE ARE NO BIRTHDAY BANNERS. I notice that as I dash through the dark kitchen, over a few piles of books and clothes, and into my bedroom, but I don't have time to care at this very second. I grab a towel off the end of the bed and lay it flat on my blanket. Then I pull the laptop out and put it carefully on the towel.

"Nonononononono," I say as I pry it open and fold the sides of the towel in. I wipe down the keyboard, but it just seems to move pockets of mud from A to L. I pull a dry corner and gently press the towel to the screen. Pock marks bloom as I pat and lift, pat and lift. Maybe I could let it dry, then scrape off the dirt? I put it in a warm spot near the window, hoping the heat will lick away some of the water. I place the ruined card next to it. Then pull out the soggy binder, and slide the Sally Ride picture out of it. I wipe it down very carefully, trying not to rip the picture in half.

"It'll be fine once it dries," I say to myself as I go to the door of the bedroom to get another towel. Really, I'm not so sure.

I'm just drying the last of the water off me when Izzy

walks in. I don't remember her leaving the house this morning wearing a crown, but now she's got one on. Not a paper crown like they would have made as a craft. It's the rim of one of those big pickle containers, but now there are little beads stuck to it.

"How was school, Izz?" I ask, tossing the towel and lifting the backpack from her shoulders.

"Well," she gives her arm a flourish, "I had to go to the principal for bossing my people!" She points her nose up in the air.

"Your people?" I say. I pull a shirt over my head and grab a pair of shorts off of the floor.

"Yes, from planet Claymon in galaxy Nomora!" Izzy says.

Queen Nomony of planet Claymon is one of our Mission Control characters. And, boy, can she be bossy.

"To the principal's office?" I say, thinking this sounds all too familiar. We head for the dining room. "Tell me the truth. Was Mrs. Sunberry one of your lieges?"

I turn and see Izzy's shoulders slump forward. "Maybe."

"Maybe?" I say, flipping on the kitchen light. Mama groans as she covers her eyes and sits up at the table. I didn't even notice her on the way in.

"Yes," Izzy confesses.

"You know you can't boss your teacher around and get away with it," I say. I go to the sink, fill up a cup of water, and set it in front of Mama. A few pieces of paper spill off the side of the table and hit the floor. I don't bother to pick them up.

"How was school?" Mama says quietly, grabbing the cup and taking a sip.

"It was fine," I say. Izzy looks at me. I raise my eyebrows.

"Jus' fine," Izzy says.

I watch as Mama puts her sunglasses on. She wedges her fingers in between the blinds and flicks them open, peering out.

"What are you looking for?" I ask.

She just grimaces and clicks her tongue. I reach for her pillbox. Her hand shoots across the table and she swipes it before I get to it. "Stop it!" She yanks it back. I let it go.

Izzy's eyes widen.

"Suit yourself," I say. "You want a sandwich?"

She has her journal out in front of her and she ignores me to write. Mama is working on something big, and if she can finish it, she'll get another job teaching; we can have a better life. Mama said as soon as she's done with her project, she's going to say good-bye to the Stop and Shop forever. She's been filling the pages of her journal a lot recently. She was writing on a laptop, until it disappeared. She said something about them bugging it and stealing her ideas. I have a feeling it is outside next to the dishes.

"Izz, why don't you go and start your homework," I say.

"I'll bring you a sandwich." She gets up and heads for the living room door.

"Goddamn government medications," Mama says. "Trying to dull me out."

"It's not that," I say, thinking that's weird for her to be saying, since last month she was saying how great she was doing with Dr. Vincent. I pull the Wonder Bread out of the bread box. I grab the mustard from the fridge and layer it on the bread.

"I have a great brain, Lucille. You don't even know!" She slams a fist on the table, sending a few more papers to the floor. Then she flicks the blind open again.

"I know, Mama," I say, sliding the mustard to the corners and back across to the other side.

"Gifted," she says.

I turn toward the sink to throw the knife into the dish bin, and take the opportunity to roll my eyes before I turn back her way. Not gifted enough to wish me a stupid happy birthday. I slap two pieces of bologna onto the bread, press another slice on top, and put it in front of her. It sits lopsided, half on a book and half off.

"Cheap, cheap," Mama grumbles, scratching her forehead.

"Well, until we win the lottery," I say.

"Win the lottery? It's rigged by the government. Taking all my money. Stopping all my cards. Goddamned go—" The word *government* dies away as she slams her journal closed and covers it with both of her hands. I want to say that the government didn't stop her cards. I want to say that she stopped her cards when she maxed them out buying crates of books from Barnes and Noble. Or when she bought the Mustang and sold the house. The government didn't have anything to do with that. Mama's looking pretty sad and I feel a twinge of guilt that I have money in the carport that she doesn't know about, but it's better to invest it into something than use it to pay off a tiny chunk of a lot of debt. I switch to a more cheery topic.

"Can you believe I'm twelve today? That we're heading out to the coast in just two days?" I start, but Mama picks up the stack of mail sitting next to her and sorts it like she doesn't even hear me. I feel a little stinger pierce the center of my belly.

Maybe she's playing at forgetting. Like she has a big surprise planned or something. A tiny voice in my head is telling me not to be stupid, but a much louder voice is saying that it's still a possibility.

I pull out four more slices of Wonder Bread. I make a bologna sandwich with mayonnaise for Izzy and one with mustard for me.

"Garbage, garbage, garbage," Mama says, sorting the bills into a pile. I watch the envelopes stack up. *Third Notice. Final Notice. Third Notice.*

It's no use stopping her right now. I run some water over the knife and put it in the dish rack.

"Ah," Mama says. "I know someone who'll be excited about this." I try to see if it's a birthday card she's holding in her hand, but she slides the envelope across the table out of sight. Then she sneaks her journal over to the side and I see her press the envelope securely between the pages.

"Well, if nothing else is going on, Izzy and I are gonna go do our homework," I say, walking toward the door.

"Yep," Mama says. "Brush up your hair, looks a mess."

"Thanks," I say, watching her put her journal into her oversized jacket pocket. She zips it up and pats it with her hand, then she looks back out the window.

"You should eat your sandwich," I say. "We'll be right in the living room if you want to join us." I swing through the door. Izzy has cleared off a spot on the coffee table, her homework packet out in front of her. First graders don't get a lot of homework, just a weekly packet. Of course, she's not doing it. Instead, she's examining her crown.

"Your feast, my queen!" I say, sliding the plate to the right and left under her nose until I drop it softly on the coffee table.

She looks up at me, eyes wide and shining. She grabs half the sandwich and takes a big bite. I pick up a half of mine and Izzy nearly spits her piece out onto the floor.

"Hold on," she says, grabbing my plate from my hand.

"Huh?" I drop the half-bitten sandwich onto the plate as she jerks it away from me.

She goes back into the kitchen. I hear doors opening and slamming.

"Are we being invaded?" Mama asks. "Are they coming for us?!"

"No," Izzy says. "Got it."

When the door swings open again, Izzy is standing there. My bologna sandwich now has a small birthday candle sticking out of it.

"Happy birthday, Lucy," she says, holding it out to me.

My heart jumps. I grab the plate. "I love it." I have a little galaxy of tears starting to form in my throat, and I swallow them down hard. "This, my queen, is the most beautiful cake I have ever laid my eyes on!"

Izzy giggles. I set it down on the coffee table and we both lean over it. Izzy pulls her pickle jar crown off her head and places it on mine. I feel the plastic scratch at my hairline.

"Don't forget a wish," Izzy says. My throat gets a little tight because that is usually Mama's line. I glance back to the door.

"In just a sec," I say, stepping over to it. I push it open a crack.

"Mama, we're going to do the birthday wish!" I say.

"Oleander seeds, the morning weeds," Mama replies. I'm not sure what that means, but I can see she's busy working something out.

I step back, letting the door slide shut, and go over to the coffee table. A little bruise blossoms right over my heart.

As I look down at my unlit candle, I'm almost certain

that birthday cake wishes are bonkers. Especially birthday cake wishes on unlit candles on bologna sandwich birthday cakes made at the Sunnyside Trailer Park, but I close my eyes and I blow out that imaginary flame on that imaginary cake. And for a second, for just a second, I let myself believe in the silliness of wishes.

Five

It's Izzy's idea to play at Mission Control later. Even though all I'm thinking about is packing, programming, and unique attributes. Still, I put my best foot forward to have some fun with her.

"Queen Nomony, are you afraid?" I sit in the driver's seat of the Mustang and start our ritual. Izzy pretends to flip switches on the dashboard.

"I'm not afraid, Cap'n," she shouts.

"And if we're to fly out into the void and become live bait for aliens, will you be afraid?" I grab hold of the wheel and duck to the right.

"I will not be afraid, sir!" She ducks to the right as well, then gets up so she is standing on her seat.

"And if we run out of fuel and have to walk through the stars until our feet bleed, will you be afraid?" I slam my foot down into the gas pedal and we race through the stars. Warp speed.

"I will not know the name of fear, Cap'n!" She gives me a sharp salute.

"And if we're taken down by space police and thrown

into a jail to be put to death by a laser-beam firing squad, will you stand with fear?"

She goes quiet and the next line is soaked with the drama of all of the space shows we have ever watched. Her hand comes down to cover her heart in a pledge. "Fear will not cross my mind nor enter my heart, Cap'n."

Cam flies through the back of the carport and does a leap into the backseat. "Then face thy doom!" He curls his arm up like he is holding a grenade launcher on his shoulder.

"Never!" Izzy shouts, raising a finger to the sky. "I may be held captive here in the Vintage Carrier, but I AM QUEEN NOMONY. I will take orders from no one. I am reclaiming this ship. I will go to Dracon and demolish . . ." Cam and I look at each other. This monologue is starting to go on a little long.

"Meet thy doom!" Cam tries again, bringing the grenade launcher to his shoulder a second time. Izzy gets the hint. She jumps down into the seat and we duck and lean back and forth, swerving around enemy ships.

Cam fires. "Boom, boom, boom! They're faster than we thought!" he shouts.

I hear the tarp crinkle and look in the rearview mirror. It's Mr. Blinks. I jump out the side of the car and go over to him.

"Hey, kiddos," Mr. Blinks says as he steps in.

"Hey, Mr. Blinks." Cam drops his imaginary grenade launcher and swivels on the back of the car.

Mr. Blinks holds out a new item. "Thought you might be able to put this to good use." It's the metal detector!

"Oh my god, you found one?" I say, as he hands it to me.

"Wasn't easy, but I did. It was this one and a bigger one. I figured the smaller one was better. How'd I do?"

I test the weight in my hand. "It's perfect," I say, laying it flat on both my palms. "Can't be more than a foot long, either."

Mr. Blinks grabs on to the side of his overalls. "Yep, I looked this item up; it's the Mini Handheld 100 and it's super lightweight."

I run my hands over the button on the base and flick it on, pointing it toward the Mustang. *Pling-tink, pling-tink,* it says. A gauge lights up as it goes over the hubcap.

"I found a couple of dimes out in the driveway with it." Mr. Blinks reaches into his pocket. "Cam here reminded me that it's your birthday." He takes my hand and puts the dimes in, folding my fingers closed.

"Thanks," I say. "I really appreciate it. Everything."

He puts his hat back on. "Least I can do." He heads back outside. I go over and set the metal detector on the desk. Daylight is fading, so I flip the light. Then hold the metal detector up against PingPing to see if the height is as good as it looks. The top of the handle will come just to the base of his head. I can't believe our good luck. I pull out a few zip ties while Cam practices backflips off of the

Mustang and Izzy goes on with her monologue. "I'll bring the catpig people with me when I leave," she says to the air. "And you will never stop me!"

A few minutes later, I hear Mr. Blinks start plucking the strings of his banjo.

"You know what that means." I turn to Izzy.

She groans and gets out of the Mustang. "Bedtime." I steer her out of the carport and lift her into our bedroom window.

"I'll be right back," I say to Cam, as I climb in after her. "Just as soon as Queen Nomony falls asleep."

"I'll be here," Cam says, positioning himself four feet back from the car.

"See if you can attach that metal detector. I left the zip ties out. Details are on the design page," I say.

"With pleasure." Cam runs for the car, flips, sort of nails the landing, and then walks over to the Mission Control station.

"Thanks." I climb in the window.

Six

Izzy slips into her pajamas and I do a quick story to get her to fall asleep. I'm about to duck out the window when I realize I better get packing. I sort through clothes, picking up shirts and sniffing the pits. Luckily, my three favorites get the all-clear. I pull a duffel out from under my bed and tuck the shirts inside. Then I choose pants and unders. I go over to Izzy's bureau, pick a few items, and pack those, too. Then I flip off the light, toss the duffel out the window. I grab the laptop and the picture of Sally Ride. Dried silt sprinkles onto the heating vent as I climb out and bring everything into the carport.

Cam is sitting at the far end, leaning close to the lamp. PingPing is now equipped with a metal spine. I go over and look closely. Cam drilled six holes in the barrel and ran zip ties through to secure the metal detector to PingPing's back, just as specified in our design. When I look at him, his football head seems like it's grinning. I push him back and forth to see how stable he is. He wobbles slightly coming back to me.

"Nice," I say. "We'll have to add a little weight in the

front to make sure our distribution is right and maybe fiddle with the trim, but I think we're close."

When Cam doesn't answer, I look down and see he is busy writing something.

"Homework?" I say, peering over his arm.

He holds up our Mission Control notebook. Page 8.

It's Cam's dream page. It's what happens after we win BotBlock. The whole page is covered with pictures and words.

Mighty Hawk: Man of Action, Man of Justice
YMCA
KARATE = brave heart
YOGA = clear mind = capacity for mind meld?
WEIGHTS = lean and mean (but only to the bad guys)

There are pictures of fists and feet flying, meditation, figures lifting weights, and something on the side with a stick figure that looks like a little old lady with a bag of groceries. Cam's going to use his half of the BotBlock money to buy a year membership to the Y. Someday, he's going to have his own gym.

Helping Kids Be Great and Getting Rid of D-Wayne Bad People, it says at the bottom. He's crossed out a bunch of mottos before. I have a feeling this one might go, too.

"That motto seems a little long . . . and, uh, personal," I say.

"I'm trying it out," he says.

I set the laptop down on the desk and sit next to him. Dirt skitters to the ground.

"Whoa, what happened there?" Cam says, wiping his hand across the laptop. He holds his silt-covered fingertips under the light.

"Destin," I say.

As he leans closer, I spot a welt on his neck, hard to detect in the shadows.

"Is that from—" I reach over and pull his collar back. It's not easy to see, but it's definitely big and it's definitely sore.

"It's fine, it's fine." He waves my hand off. "I'm much faster than him for the most part. Did Destin throw mud at you or something?"

"Cam . . ."

"Seriously. You should have seen that fool face-plant trying to catch me. No one gets Mighty Hawk."

D-Wayne gets Mighty Hawk, I think, but I don't say it 'cause I can see he isn't interested in talking about it. Cam has been cursed with blind optimism. I don't know how or why, but he has it. He says all the action heroes carry the optimism gene, otherwise they'd have nothing to fight for and they'd go down easy.

"Looks like *you* could have used my help, though," he says.

"First of all, I held my own." Then I tell him what happened, from leaving the classroom, through the bologna sandwich birthday cake wishes. "No laptop, no programming for the Rescue Mission." I look away from Gram's searching gaze. "And we're running out of time."

"Could we just do the RC part?" Cam starts and I cut him off.

"You know we can't. If we don't program, we only do two competitions. And if we only do two competitions, we don't qualify for the all around—"

He starts nodding before I even finish. "Right, right, no all around, no prize money."

Cam pulls the race specs out of the back of the Mission Control notebook.

I pull the laptop close to me and blow on the keyboard. The dirt and silt fluffs toward the monitor. Cam closes the Mission Control binder and puts it out of the way of the dust.

I press the power button.

Nothing.

Cam makes a crackling sound with his voice. "Captain Juniper Ray, this is Mighty Hawk. We've got no response."

I grab the cord. There's an outlet on the outside of the trailer. "I hear you, over. Testing with power. Commencing now."

I push the plug in and press the power button again. A little light flicks on. And the keyboard lights up.

"We've got power!" I say.

We slap five. Words flash across the screen, but blink out before I can read them. I wait, crossing my fingers. But it freezes on the black screen.

"We'll just give it a minute," I say.

"Yeah, it always needs a minute to boot up," Cam says. He twirls a pencil in between his fingers, hits a beat on the edge of the desk.

A minute goes by. Two minutes go by. A tiny whisper seems to come from the keys and both Cam and I lean in. The laptop makes a crackling sound.

"Uh, that's not good!" Cam shouts. He lets go of the pencil and it sails over his right shoulder.

I grab the cord and yank it out of the wall. The crackle dies with a pop and the laptop lies still. I pick it up and examine it underneath the lamp. A little wisp of smoke filters up out of the keys. The battery pack is very warm on my fingers.

"Great," I say. "It's officially fried."

"Just borrow another laptop tomorrow?" Cam says.

"Really? Do you really think she'll let me borrow another one if this is what happens? Oh god." My mind races. "I'll probably have to buy a new one. We can't buy a new one!"

"Hold on, now, Cap'n, you're panicking. We gotta think it through." Cam gets up and paces back and forth next to the Mustang. Cam always seems to think better on his feet.

"I mean, you're smart, Cap'n, but in this case, you'd be better off thinking like someone outside the law. First of all, it's almost the end of the school year. All this junk"—he gestures toward the laptop—"is getting real worn out, anyway."

"Maybe, but most of it's not filled with mud," I say, scraping a piece of grass off of the bottom with my fingernail. "Most of it's salvageable."

"Still, we have to evaluate our options."

"Okay, option one: I explain what happened and she doesn't let me take another laptop out. Option two: I have to pay for it and she still doesn't let me take another one out. Option three: I have to pay for it and maybe she'll let me take another one out, but with conditions."

"Option four," he turns, heads back in my direction. "You bring it to school under the radar, don't mention anything is wrong, and then once she notices, halfway through summer, she'll think it just burned out!"

I rub my hands over my eyes. I'm liking option four, but not so sure it's a foolproof plan.

"We just place it back in the laptop cart nonchalantly and take out another one. Make the change on the sign-out sheet to cover our tracks. It's a simple old switcheroo." He crosses his arms and leans up against the Mustang.

"I think it looks suspicious, especially with the mud . . . situation. I'm the one that checks them out the most. If one is sitting in there caked in mud, she is going to come to me first. She probably won't even check the sign-out sheet."

I lean down close to the keys and blow again. More dirt comes out, but when I press the keys they crackle and pop underneath my fingertips. "Maybe if we had something to pump all the dirt out, so it looks like the others."

Cam snaps. "Can air."

"Can air?" I say. "Can air what?"

"*Can* air. I've seen Mrs. Shareze use it on her keyboard. It's like a spray bottle filled with air." He holds his hand up like he is holding up a can of WD-40. "Pshhh, pshhh. You know?"

I jump up. "*Compressed* air!" I shout. "I've seen it, too." My fingers tingle.

Cam comes over and picks up the laptop. "Easy," he says. "She always has her coffee in the teachers' lounge before the bell, so her room should be empty."

"All right." I lick my lips. "I could just get there early." Gram peers at me from the picture frame and I have to turn it slightly so she isn't looking into my eyes. I turn back to Cam. "I could get the compressed air and clean it all up so that it's in tip-top shape."

"And then we slide it on home." He sails the laptop through the air like a magic carpet, then sets it down, grabs another pencil from the jar at the edge of my make-shift desk, and starts using that one as a drumstick, too. *Ditditditdit bingbing,* onto the edge of the lamp. "While you're cleaning that one, I'll check out the new one. Fool-proof."

If we want to program PingPing tomorrow, if we really want to compete, we don't have a choice. "Just as long as we're there early."

A wail comes from the trailer next door and Cam drops his eyes, shaking his head. "Let's just hope I get some sleep."

"Camrin?" That'd be his sister Judy.

"I'll see you first thing," Cam says as he heads toward the back of the carport.

"Okay," I say. "T-minus twenty-one hours until liftoff and T-minus sixty hours until competition." I'm starting to have my doubts that this was meant to be.

"I think you mean T-minus sixty hours until the road to victory," Cam says.

"I hope so," I answer, crossing my fingers that he's right about that.

"Oh." He pulls the tarp aside and a second later reappears with a backpack. "Almost forgot." He dumps the bag into the back of the Mustang. "All packed and ready to go!"

"Right," I say, looking at PingPing. "All ready, except for the most important part."

"Nothing can be done tonight," Cam says. "But we'll get it tomorrow."

"Camrin?" Judy says again.

"I better run." He ducks out of the carport.

I secure two bolts to the bottom of the frame to even out the weight of the metal detector. Then I flip the RC on and adjust the trim and do one practice run. PingPing is doing better than ever. After that, I get restless thinking I still have a million things to prepare for. I start sifting through junk parts. I sort some into a bin to bring along. A couple extra servos in case PingPing ends up with a burned-out joint, and plenty of extra wire for mishaps of other kinds. I put the soldering iron in, too. I pick up an old microphone bag that Mr. Blinks brought me. This is going to be my Mission Control Important Items Bag. I take a Sharpie from the desk and scribble the initials on the front of it, *MCIIB,* then toss the Sharpie inside. I pull the desk drawer open and take out my USB-compatible transmitter. I place it delicately into the soft lining. Then I take out the only other item in the drawer: a printed registration form. I fold it and tuck it underneath the transmitter. What else will I need with me for the big day? Of course, I'll have the laptop and the remote control. Scanning the desk, I take an extra battery pack off the charger. Then I pick up the picture of Gram, give it a kiss, and tuck it into the bag, too. Last, I bring the MCIIB over to the car, unzip my duffel bag, and place it inside. I survey the area. All clear. I go back over to my Mission Control station and flip our notebook open to the Protocol for Optimum Achievement.

I write in one middle step.

1.5) Swap out laptop

I pull the Sally Ride picture from the corner of the desk where I dropped it. It's all dry now, just crumpled and covered in silt. I spread it flat and dust some mud off her face. Then I pull a glue stick out of the pencil holder and use the very last bit of glue to secure the picture to the front of our Mission Control book. Smoothing the corners, I press on all sides so there's no chance of it falling off. Just a few more steps, a few easy steps, and we're headed for the stars. That's what I tell myself. I press my hand over it one more time so I can go to bed believing.

Seven

"MAMA?" IZZY'S VOICE BREAKS THROUGH MY dreams and I pull my eyes open. It's not morning. I know that right away. The room is pitch black.

"Mama, is that you?" Izzy asks.

I shoot straight up and swing around so I'm facing the center of the room. Mama is in the doorway and she is pulling a long-sleeved shirt over her head. She flicks the light switch and I shield my eyes as the room flares to life.

"What time is it?" I say, trying to blink my eyes clear so I can see my watch. They finally focus and I groan.

"It's one thirty," I say. When I drop my hand, I see Mama adjusting her sunglasses on her face.

"Burning my brain out," she says.

"No kidding," I say, pushing my covers off.

Mama walks to Izzy's bed and lifts her into an upright position.

"What's going on?" I ask, afraid I already know the answer.

"We're going for a ride," she says, taking a sweater off of the knob on Izzy's headboard.

"It's the middle of the night, Mama. Izzy and I need to sleep for school tomorrow."

She helps Izzy into the sweater and fumbles with the top button. "Not tonight. It's the only safe time to go out." She shakes her head, stands up, and unzips her oversized pocket as Izzy puts her buttons together. Mama pulls out her notebook and slides something out of the front cover.

"It's what I've been looking for. It was there all along." She stuffs the book back into her pocket real fast and zips it in, then waves the piece of paper in front of me. I grab hold of her wrist so I can see the print. It's that poem she pulled out of the book earlier today.

"Mama, we really need to get to sleep," I say, tucking my feet back into bed. "We gotta get up in the morning. Clean up. Pack your bag."

"Hey, please," Mama says. She grabs hold of the blankets before I can pull them up. "Can you look at me?"

I keep my eyes trained on the blanket. "Can you look at me please? What's the harm?"

I look up at her masked eyes. "The harm is being tired for school tomorrow," I say. Especially since I have to get the laptop back and program PingPing and everything. "The harm is not being prepared to leave for the coast. We have to rest up. We have a long weekend ahead of us."

"We'll be fine." She releases the blanket. "We have the rest of the night. We're just going to watch the northern lights. I happened along this poem and they're connected." She sits down at the end of Izzy's bed. "Serendipity. Never let it pass you by. Would you like to see the northern lights, baby girl?"

"What's a northern light?" Izzy asks, putting her thumb in her mouth. She's too old for that, but I'm going to let it slide 'cause she's probably nervous.

"It's like the sky is being colored with all your favorite watercolors. You want to see it. Oh, Izzy, it's magic!"

Izzy giggles. "I want to."

I groan. "No, no, no," I say.

"Yes, yes, yes!" Mama says, singing the last yes so it echoes through the quiet of the night. I turn and slam my window closed. Last thing I need is everyone seeing Mama go off the deep end.

"I'm going to call Doctor Vincent," I say.

Mama's smile slides off her face. "Nope. You're not." She points at me. "You, party pooper, can go back to bed. Izzy and I'll go out and watch the northern lights. If you can't have a little fun, maybe we should stay home this weekend."

"What?" Party pooper? Where's the party? I want to yell. It's obviously not for me. I groan and get out of bed. "Fine," I say, pulling a sweatshirt on.

"Yeah, yeah." Mama stands up and I see her step to the side and catch herself. I wonder if it's her brain or if she's been drinking. Either way, I don't think she should be driving us around.

"Let's go!" Mama staggers toward the bedroom door, then starts giggling.

We'll just go out and come right back. I'll get some sleep and be ready to go to school early. I'll call Dr. Vincent first thing in the morning and let him know that Mama's doing midnight rides again. But not so much that he'll worry about us going on the trip. It'll all be okay.

I pull some sweat pants on over my shorts. Mama is already bustling down the narrow hallway to the back door, and every few steps I hear a thump as she careens into the wall. We step into the hallway and Izzy runs to catch up, her white nightie billowing out at her heels. Mama starts giggling again halfway down the hallway.

"We have to be quiet. People are trying to sleep," I hiss. *Please be quiet. Please don't wake up the whole park.*

Mama stifles her giggle as we get to the door, and she crouches down like she's sneaking out. Izzy giggles, too, and we head into the night air. The stars are full bright in the sky. We duck into the carport and Mama goes around to the other side of the car, the passenger side.

"Mama, I can't drive," I say. This isn't true. Gram taught me how to drive the Mustang soon as she could after we were left at the general store. I glance toward the duffel bag where her picture is hidden, and hear her with me.

You stay in control. You have control of the car at all times. Go as slow as you need to.

I grab the handle and think how she made me drive up and down the lane of the trailer park over and over and over until I had it.

"Can you please," Mama says, waving toward the driver's seat. She opens her side door and gets in. I sigh, slide in, too, and push the brake. *Press the brake, push the car into reverse. Always have the brake all the way in when shifting.*

I open my hand and Mama presses the keys into it. I rattle the house key away and put the car key into the ignition.

The door slams and I give Izzy a glare in the backseat. "Let's keep it down, okay?"

Mama must not hear me because she raises her face to the roof and shouts, "'I have been one acquainted with the night.'"

I snap a look at her, too. "Shhhh," I say, but it's too late. A baby's wail sails out of the McKinneys' window, just beyond the carport. I see a light flick on, splashing a blue haze over us. A muddy halo erupts around Mama's head. I'm sure Cam's awake now.

"'I have walked out in rain,'" Mama says, holding her poem up to her nose.

"You're going to wake the whole park," I hiss.

"Then get going and stop being such a whiner!" she says. "I'll do it again, I'll dazzle Sunnyside Trailer Park with the perfection that is Robert Frost poetry." She waves the piece of paper at me. I realize the carport is still closed, so I jump out and hurry to the back, grab the edge of the tarp, and roll it as quick as I can from one side to the other. I secure it with a bungee cord. Then I run back to the driver's seat and get in.

Make sure your seat and mirrors are in place, I hear Gram say as I reach underneath the seat for the adjustment bar. I pull it forward until I can push the brake all the way in. I look over at Mama, who is rifling around in her purse. For a minute, she looks just like Gram. I picture us in our first driving lesson as we passed by Mr. Sikes's porch.

You're going to end up in the looney bin again for this one! he shouted as we slipped by.

I'll see you there, Harold, Gram said, adjusting her glasses on her nose. She didn't miss a beat. Not ever.

I turn the key as Mama pulls lipstick out of her purse and starts applying it. The Mustang roars to life.

"Buckle up," I say quietly, and I look in the rearview mirror to see Izzy grab her seat belt and pull it around her. I do the same.

"Live a little, darling," Mama says, leaving hers un-hooked. I roll my eyes.

"Suit yourself." I hold the wheel. *Ten o'clock and two o'clock.*

"Where are we going?" I say.

"Head out toward 32 and then take a left on Trunkton Road, please." Mama makes a pop sound with her lips and I hear the clip of the cap going back onto her lipstick.

I grab the gearshift and pull it so the arrow clicks into alignment with R. Reverse. Then I put my hand on the back of Mama's seat, turn around, and steer the car out of the carport. It's straight back so that's the easiest kind of reversing. Don't move the wheel at all, just release the brake a little and take it slow.

The car does a lot of jolting and jerking at first, but then slides smooth all the way out. I push the brake and take a breath. Then I move the gearshift to the D and go nice and slow between the trailers. A few lights are on, and I duck down in case people are peering out of their windows at this time of night. I slouch a little extra as we pass Mrs. Barlow's house.

"'I have been one acquainted with the night,'" Mama says, resting her head on the seat. She takes a deep sigh like this is some special moment. I slow down at the end of the lane and turn right onto Route 5.

"'I have walked out in rain—and back in rain. I have outwalked the furthest city light.'"

I keep my eyes on the road and concentrate on not grinding my teeth.

"That's where we're going," Mama says. "Out past the furthest city light, to see the vastness of the sky."

I squeeze the steering wheel and focus on getting us there and back safe. I take a right onto Fielders Lane and we drive through town. It's dead quiet and I wonder what it is like in some of these houses. I bet kids are snug in their beds, tucked in with stuffed animals and plush pillows. Hours into their sweet dreams.

Halfway through town, Mama grabs hold of the knob on the radio. She flicks her wrist and music peels through the sky. I grab the knob as fast as I can while still trying to keep the car on the right side of the yellow line and silence it.

"Live a little, daughter," Mama says, circling her hands around and around in the air. Her bangle bracelets click together and slide down her arms. I see Izzy in the rearview mirror. Her hands fly up, palms toward the sky. I'm not sure what is so fun about this, but she seems to be enjoying it.

We pass the sign that says Pendleton and on into Parkview. We're long past the last city light and Mama still hasn't told me exactly where we're going, when I see a lick of color on the horizon. I catch my breath.

"You saw it!" Mama says, grabbing my shoulder and shaking. "You saw it!"

"I don't know," I say, as the horizon slides behind a hill and we descend into a dip. When we come back up, Izzy is centered in the middle of our seats. When I glance in the rearview mirror, I see her mouth open, eyes searching, hair flying out and up in the wind. We sail back up the other side of the dip. My stomach sinks and jounces. Mama makes a "whoooooooooo!" as we head up the hill. I cringe as her voice splits through the night, sailing into the wind and silencing the peepers.

I push the gas pedal down as we begin to lose momentum, rising up, up, up. The sky begins to come into view, a panorama slide show, unfolding before our eyes. For a moment, the only color I see is the yellow line in the middle of the road, but once I get to the top, there it is. Green, blue, purple flashes of light licking the belly of the sky.

I slam on the brake as I realize I'm paying more attention to the lights than to the road. The tires squeal on the asphalt. Mama jumps out of the car before it has completely stopped. We slide sideways.

"Mama, wait!" I shout, realizing we've pulled off right next to Sanctum Lake. I jam the car into park. We jolt to a standstill. Gram would be after me about not being at a complete and final stop for that one, but I don't have time to worry about it.

"Izzy, stay on my tail," I say as I jump out of the car. Izzy falls in right behind me and we light out after Mama, who is running up a grassy knoll.

"That's a good place to stop!" I shout, trying to get my feet moving faster.

"Wait up!" Izzy shouts and I reach back to grab her hand. It's damp from her thumb being stuck in her mouth. I only look down long enough to take my hand out of hers and wipe the spit off on the hem of my shirt, but as I look back up, Mama's disappeared over the top of the hill.

"Hurry!" I hiss. We run through the grass, which bends and whips with the light breeze. I get to the top of the knoll, my eyes searching for Mama. She's a moving shadow, but then as the moon comes out from behind a quickly passing cloud, she appears like a lost patch of stardust. Her white nightgown ripples silver in the moonlight. Her bracelets pop, sparkling threads crisscrossing her arm.

The gray streaks in her hair become shining cobwebs, holding her curls in place all the way down her back. She slows as she gets to the edge of the lake.

"Mama!" My heart hits my throat, wondering what she is thinking and if it's safe for her to be near the water. Dr. Vincent says evaluate the situation. Is she going to harm others? I don't think so. Is she going to harm herself? I don't know. If the answer is yes, then I have to call 911. Course, I don't have a phone. I look down at Izzy as she pops her thumb back in her mouth.

"You don't need to be doing that," I mumble and she yanks it out, rolling her eyes at me. I watch Mama as she holds her arms to each side, and a shiver runs up my back as she lifts one leg straight out in front of her. Like a dancer, she slowly lowers her foot toward the water, and then through the surface.

"Mama, what are you doing? You probably should come back here!" I shout. The breeze lifts my hair and whips it in front of my eyes and across my cheeks.

But she doesn't answer. She just steps in. One foot, and then the other. And she turns to face me, and she falls back. For a moment, I panic and start running down the hill. The grass grabs at my feet, but I'm moving fast enough that the blades get pulled straight from the roots. I hit the sand and she breaks through the surface. I slide to a stop. Izzy crashes into me and I sprawl forward. A belly flop on the edge of the lake. Mouth full of sand. Mama sprays water into the sky and smiles. Then she bobs along on her back, clothes soaked through. And laughs. I pick myself up. Wipe the grit from my mouth. My insides feel like I swallowed a handful of bare, frayed wires. Sharp and stingy from the bottom of my ribs to the backs of my eyes.

I hold Izzy's hand, and I watch Mama. The ripples around her reflect the starry sky. Bouncing strands of color collide with the stars and dance with one another. She floats along the surface, a pearl silhouette in a magical pool. I feel my breath get caught in my throat. Her clothes are so wet that I can see all her parts. My mind starts to race. I look out toward the road, thinking, *please don't let anyone come by.* Thinking, *I wouldn't call 911 now if I had to.* Thinking, *cover up. What are you doing? Why are you doing this? Why aren't we asleep in bed like the other kids?*

"I can see through her nightie," Izzy says, squeezing my hand.

"Let's keep an eye on the lights," I say. "We'll go home soon."

I lead Izzy over to the grass, out of the sightline of the road. If someone does come by, maybe we can sneak into the woods, just over there.

Along the tender breeze, I hear Mama's voice, calling us to join her.

"Come on, girls, come and swim." She splashes and then starts going over that Robert Frost poem again. "'One luminary clock against the sky'—come on, girls, isn't it the most perfect thing you've ever heard? It's the moon of course."

Shut up, I want to scream. Shut up with your stupid poem. But instead I take a deep breath and cross my legs and make sure I'm a good distance out of the sightline of the road.

Izzy climbs into my lap, her big eyes still facing the sky. And I tell myself to look up, too. Don't watch Mama, don't listen. Just watch the stars. Still, I hear her happiness float up from the water to the sky and for a second I wish I were a part of it. I wish I could get even close to that kind of happy. Here on my birthday night, I search the constellations, from Orion, to the Big Dipper, to his little brother, straight down to the Milky Way. Wondering if I might find it, also.

"I'm getting tired," Izzy says, as she buries her face in my shirt.

"Me too," I say. "Me too."

Eight

As we head back down the dip, Mama starts to get quiet. And by the time we're back to the house she rushes inside and straight into her room. Closing the door without so much as a hug good night. I open the linen closet and pull the last towel off of the shelf.

"Mama," I say, knocking gently on the door. "You probably should dry off."

I hear a noise from the other side of the door, shuffling, moving, but no answers.

"Lucy, I'm going to bed. I'm really tired," Izzy says through a yawn.

"Okay," I say. "Go ahead." Izzy ducks into our room. I turn and knock on Mama's door. "Mama, you're soaked through." I tilt my head and listen. No response. I turn the knob and step into her dark room. I scan her bed, barely lit by the light spilling in from outside. She isn't there. Just piles of clothes. I go over to the closet. Not there. I turn to the right. She's in the nook. The little spot in the corner between her bed and the wall. A chair closes it off into a little square. She's lying there with her pillow under her head.

"Mama, you okay?" I ask, looking over the chair.

"I'm fine. We'll be fine. All fine," she says, softly. "Just be quiet please. I don't feel well."

I glance over at her nightstand. The clock reads 3:00 a.m. "Maybe we should call—"

Mama flips over real fast. "I said I'm fine. Promise me you won't. I'll feel better once I sleep."

I hold out the towel.

"What's this?" she says.

"A towel," duh, "for you to dry off with. You're soaked."

She takes it. "Right, right. I know." She wipes her chin and wraps it around her head.

"Will you pass me another pillow?" Mama says. I reach across the bed and grab her second pillow. She takes it and places it underneath her head along with the first. She closes her eyes and I see her tremble.

"You need a blanket," I say, pulling one off her bed. All of the clothes on top of it fall to the floor. I bring the blanket over and cover her with it. She keeps her eyes going left to right and left to right. And her mouth dips down, getting sad, sad, sad. Her spaceship is crashing.

"Sleep tight," I say.

"Right," Mama says, flipping back to the wall.

I go toward the door, stepping over piles of clothes and shoes, out into the hallway. I slide the door shut behind me but it stops about a hand's length from the door frame. Jammed. I look down. A shoe, shirt, papers. I try to push them with my foot, but they don't budge. I lean down and grab hold of the shirt and yank. It gets caught on the edge and then sends the shoe catapulting into the wall behind me.

"What was that!" Mama shouts. I open the door to see her sitting back up, looking around. "Was that a gunshot!?"

"No," I say, clearing the door frame. "Just a shoe. You're fine."

"I'm fine," Mama says, disappearing below the edge of the bed.

I slide the door closed, this time smoothly. As I walk back toward my room, I kick a shirt out of the way. There's something white and rectangular underneath it.

I sink to the floor. It looks a little like a birthday card. I pick it up. It's definitely a card of some sort. But I can barely see a thing here in the hallway. I step back past Mama's room to the back door so I'm standing in a ray of moonlight. I press my finger along the seal. It hasn't been stuck closed, so it doesn't need any tearing to get it open. I slide the card out of the envelope.

For my daughter, on her birthday, it says on the front underneath a vase of flowers. I flip the card open.

You're the best daughter I could ever imagine. I'm so proud of you, the glossy writing shines in the light. And I wince. I wince 'cause it's Hallmark mumbo jumbo. Mama didn't even sign it. It just says *LOVE,* in her messy handwriting. Like she obviously had other things to do besides sign a card for her stupid kid. I throw it back over my shoulder. It belongs on the floor. Love comma. Stupid. My eyes fill up with tears as I make my way to bed. I don't let them squeeze out. The tears just sit on the surface like they're making a new home there. I tell myself to sleep. But it doesn't happen. Instead, my mind rewinds to other midnight birthday surprises. Better ones.

My eighth birthday. Our first year in Seahook. While Gram put Izzy to bed, Mama and I ate popcorn and Starbursts from the vending machine. And Mama let me run the remote. I watched Star Wars, *the originals, and pigged out while lounging on the hotel bed. But as the clock switched from 11:39 to 11:40 and the* Star Wars *episode came to a close, Mama got up and looked out the window.*

"I think we better get out to the beach now," Mama whispered, "so we can make it there for your birthday."

I slid out of bed and into my shoes, pulling the Velcro across. Mama picked up a bag and her purse.

"What's that?" I whisper, thinking it looked something like birthday surprises.

"Oh, nothing important," Mama said, but I could tell from her smile and her sideways look that she was being sneaky. I thought about what it might be as I pulled a Windbreaker on over my pajamas. Maybe that stuffed turtle I saw at the tourist shop on the pier today. Maybe something else. You never knew with Mama.

"What's going on?" Gram muttered as one eye half opened.

"Nothing," Mama said, "just heading down to the beach

to celebrate Lucy's birthday before the rest of the world wakes up."

Gram nodded and muttered her way back into dreams.

Mama snuck the door open and we tiptoed down the hallway and out into the fresh night air. I heard the sounds of the ocean. I jumped up onto the sidewalk and walked the edge of it like it was a balance beam. Mama saw me doing it and she got in behind me and did the same as we made our way down Ocean Avenue. "Listen to the sea, Lucy! What's it saying?" she asked as she balance-stepped behind me.

I listened to the waves roll in and out and in and out, and the water gush up against itself. Hushhushhushhush. Whushwhushwhushwhush. I stepped to the beat, felt it in my heart. Felt it in my legs and in my toes.

"RunRunRunRun," I said, jumping off of the sidewalk. Jumping high like it might blast me off into space.

"Is it?" Mama said, stopping to cock her ear. I landed and listened, too.

Mama nodded. "So it is." She turned, but before she could get going, I darted out in front of her, knowing exactly what she was going to do, knowing exactly which way she would go. Mama and I sped down the sidewalk. The shadows and cement peeled away into sand, sea, and stars as we hit the beach and went to meet the waves. I slipped and slid in the sand and had to stop to take my shoes off. I left them propped against the stone wall lining the beach.

We ran along, kicking the waves. Smashing them to smithereens. I got fifteen before my toe scraped along something and when I looked down I saw the curve of a blue shell. I reached down and picked it up, wondering if it really was blue. It had a sort of glow to it.

"They turn blue at night because they suck up the moonlight," Mama said, like she was reading my mind. She picked up another and handed it to me. I watched the two shells tuck together like wings in the palm of my hand. "But they're white in the morning. Aren't they?"

"Well," Mama said. "The magic's gone by then. The daylight sucks it out."

The shells seemed to shift in my hand. Moving on their own to prove that they were genuine pieces of magic.

Mama sat down and pulled the surprise bag onto her lap. I settled into the sand cross-legged and pretended I didn't notice what she was doing. Instead, I watched the Milky Way. I stared at it, thinking it looked like it was made up of more than just stars. Like maybe a lady named Captain Milky Way picked up the sand and moon shells from earth. Only on her way into deep space, her ship sprung a leak, sprinkling the heavens with a trail of magic.

A second later, I heard a lighter spark and Mama's face lit up with an amber glow. I sat up on my knees. A candle and cupcake floated up from the bag. Mama cupped it between her hands, and where her fingers landed, the frosting began. It looked like a little cloud with a candle on top.

"Make a wish, baby girl."

I thought on it for a minute. Everything seemed perfect here. Me and Mama sitting in the middle of the sand. A glow-

ing little orb of orange surrounding us in the blue-soaked night.

"Do you want a great year in third grade? Or a new bike? Or maybe a new stuffed animal?" Mama looked up to the sky. "A piece of the Milky Way?" she joked. But I looked down into my hand and seeing I already had a piece of it, a piece of the magic, I made a wish for nothing to ever change. I blew out the candle and the little orange orb disappeared into a jagged smoky line between us.

I ate the sticky cupcake, chocolate frosting over straw-berry. Mama had one, too. And we sat and watched the stars. She did get me that stuffed animal from the pier and I col-lected a jar full of moon shells and we swam and called to the sky and Mama read a poem about a cow thinking the Milky Way was his pasture.

But sometimes birthday wishes get botched. Sometimes it just takes a while to realize that it's all hocus-pocus. That there isn't any magic. That moon shells are just lost pieces of mollusks and clams, not related to the Milky Way at all. I hear doors opening and closing. Mama must be up. I don't get out of bed to check on her. I spot that old jar of moon shells on my desk. Then flip away from it, toward the window, toward the carport. I try to think on real things right here in this world. Things like plans and promises, making choices, and BotBlock. As much as I try to think about steps one, two, and three, the memory plays over and over again in the background. And I fall asleep with a wanting in my heart.

Nine

I KNOW WE'RE LATE BEFORE I even pull my eyes open. I know because I heard Chuck making his racket, but it got wrapped into dreams. And when I finally wake, it's silent. He's done his song for the day.

Thwak, thwak, thwak. I flip over and look out at Cam's face. Big bags have piled up under his eyes and he looks at me with something that is the opposite of Mighty Hawk. Zero Energy Man, maybe. He holds the laptop up. Some dust filters down. I look at my watch and Cam says it at the same time as I see it. "It's seven fifty-five."

I groan. School just started.

I pull the window open. My arms are still heavy with sleep, but I manage it. As it slides up, only one word seems right for the moment.

"Crap," I say, eyeing the brightening sky over the park behind Cam.

"You can say that again." He rubs the back of his hand over his eyes.

He looks up at me, then gestures toward the laptop. "Maybe we can make the switch during lunch?"

"Yeah, we better," I say, thinking my options are depleting. Getting critically low now. "I'll meet you in ten."

"I'll write the notes." He walks toward the carport.

I pull Izzy out of bed. "We gotta jet to school!" She opens her eyes and slumps into me.

"No, thank you," she says. But I manage to get her dressed. It is not an easy feat to get a grumpy queen dressed first thing in the morning.

I pull a sweatshirt over my head, throw on some jeans, and we walk through the living room. Mama is sitting hunched on the couch. Her face is down in her hands. Great.

Gram had a name for this. Meditation of Misery. It's what sadness looks like. Everything is turning down into a frown. Shoulders bend, smiles slide off faces. My first thought is *uh-oh*. My second is that she'd better snap out of this by the time we have to leave for the BotBlock later today, or nothing else will matter. Not the laptop, not our plans, not my promise to Gram, none of it.

"I'm calling Dr. Vincent, Mama," I say as I pass. She doesn't respond. I don't need her to.

I step around piles of books until I'm out in the kitchen. I grab Izzy's backpack off the hook near the door and hand it to her.

"You go and meet Cam at the carport, tell him I'll be right there."

She moseys outside. I notice the rat's nest of knots at the back of her head and make a mental note to get some of

73

that out before school if I can. I grab the phone off the hook, take a deep breath, and pull the little piece of paper off the bulletin board. I step out onto the tiny porch so Mama can't hear me, then dial the numbers and listen.

Ring ring . . . Ring ring . . . Ring ring. It rings three times, then there's a crackle on the line.

You have reached the office of Dr. Vincent. If this is a life-threatening emergency, please hang up and dial 911. If this isn't an emergency, please leave your name, number, and a brief message and I'll return your call as soon as I can. Have a good day.

Beep!

"Uh, hey, Dr. Vincent, this is Lucille Peevey. I'm calling 'cause, uh, she looks pretty down this morning. I didn't know if you guys had your meeting or appointment or whatever. I didn't know if her medication changed. Uh, anyway, not an emergency, but call us. Bye."

I click end and go inside, placing the phone in the receiver. My stomach growls, so I head toward the fridge. I pull the door open and look for something that might work for breakfast. Seems everything but actual food is in the fridge. There's a notepad sitting on the top shelf next to the ketchup. A knife in the upper corner, hiding behind a bottle of orange juice. I pull it out and drop it into the sink so that no one gets cut on it. I spot two browning bananas hanging off a hook on the counter, so I slam the fridge closed, grab those, and get going.

When I get into the carport, Cam jumps off the desk and

hands me the laptop. I take it and put it into my backpack.

"Let's do this," Cam says, pulling two folded notes from his pocket. "From Mrs. Margaret Peevey. All in caps, just like your mama."

I take the note and slide it into my pocket. "Izzy?" I spot her snarled hair on the other side of the car. I walk around and see she is writing in the sand with a stick.

"Can you get me a rubber band?" I ask Cam as I take her hair and start maneuvering it into a ragged ponytail. Cam searches the desk and a second later the rubber band wings over my shoulder and hits the tarp.

"Really?" I say, holding the ponytail with one hand and reaching for it with the other.

"Fastest way to get it to you, Cap'n," Cam says.

I shake the rubber band free of dirt and secure the ponytail the best I can.

"Rat's nest," I mutter, looking up at Cam.

"It'll do," he says.

"Wait," Izzy says, unzipping her backpack. She pulls her pickle jar crown out of it and puts it on her head so her ponytail is rising up out of the center. Then she zips her backpack up like all is well and heads out of the carport. Cam and I follow. I look back toward the trailer, wondering if maybe I should stay, but I know how this works. Mama's not going to move for a while. Could be hours. Dr. Vincent will call or come by and it'll be okay. We'll be in tip-top shape tonight. And we can leave for BotBlock as planned. Dr. Vincent will fix everything.

Since we've already missed the bus, we walk down to Cherry Lane Elementary first. It starts to sprinkle halfway there, and I look up, wondering why the sky even has to spit on me when things are going so awful.

We drop Izzy at the door of the elementary school and I watch as she makes her way straight down the hall and into her classroom. The hall monitor looks over at her and frowns. I can see she is looking at Izzy's hair. And judging it, too. It's going to be a long day.

Cam and I go two blocks over, not talking much. I look down at my watch. Eight thirty. I press the mode and it switches to the timer.

"T-minus nine hours until liftoff," I say as we head into the school. "And forty-eight hours until competition."

"Don't despair, yet, Cap'n," Cam says as we head into the office. A lady cuts in front of us, setting her bag up on the counter.

"Hi, I'm Sharon Clementine. I'm here as the sub for"— she looks down at her piece of paper—"uh, Mrs. Shareze?"

I risk a look at Cam. We lock eyes.

"Yes, thanks for coming in on such short notice, Sharon," Mrs. Ginesh—the secretary—says. "Please sign in. Here's your visitor's badge. Head down to room 221. Principal Partridge is down there currently and will give you a quick rundown of what needs to happen today."

Mrs. Clementine scribbles on a clipboard and then grabs her bag and heads down the hall. We step up to the counter.

"My, we're all running late today, it seems," Mrs. Ginesh says. You don't know the half of it, lady, I think, but we hand her the notes Cam made. She glances back and forth. Looks like she might question them, but I guess decides it isn't worth it. She initials them and hands them back. "Please report to your classroom."

"Thanks, Mrs. G," Cam says. And we head out the door.

I wait until we're out of sight of the main office before I turn to Cam. "Mrs. Shareze's out." I think of her cold yesterday. It must've gotten worse.

"I can't believe it," he says as we pass the overly cheery mural of kids holding hands.

"This is going to work," I say. "We just need to find a time to get in when the sub isn't there."

"Maybe at the end of the day?" Cam says. "Subs usually leave as fast as possible."

It could work. We turn the corner and come to room 221. Principal Partridge comes out the door and we nod and hold out our notes so she knows there's no funny business. She just hurries past us. We hang up our bags and take our seats.

"Hello, class, I'm Mrs. Clementine, your teacher for today," she says as she spells out her name on the board. As she makes a final flourish at the end of her name, I can't help but feel a little bit of gratitude. Even the sky out the classroom window has a little ray of light splitting through a cloud.

Ten

THE BELL RINGS. WE LINE UP with the rest of the herd and head out toward the front doors. My hands seem to be jumping around on their own. Snapping and tapping my legs and acting all suspicious. I jam them in my pockets to keep them still. As we pass the water fountain I stop.

"Hang here," I say. Cam slips out of line, too. He leans over and starts sucking down water while I stand against the wall. Once he's had his fill, I get some. Then we take time staring at the cheery mural and let the halls empty out a little bit. Just as most of the kids are leaving, just as I'm about to give up hope all together, Mrs. Clementine walks out of 221 and heads toward the office.

"Now, Cap'n?" Cam whispers.

"Let me go first," I say, "then you follow in two minutes."

I grip the strap of my pack and head back to the classroom. I look both ways before I slide the door open again and step in. Mrs. Shareze isn't going to like this when she gets in tomorrow morning. What a mess. I pick up a crumpled piece of paper and chuck it in the garbage as I head for her desk. I step around it and look at the tables and chairs. The whole room is different from this angle. It's kind of like a captain's control station. I scan the top of the desk for some compressed air. A notepad with some random scribbles sits to one side. Her computer is off, and there's a calendar resting right below her keyboard. She has multicolored Post-it notes everywhere. Worksheets we did today sit next to a letter from the sub.

The door opens and I dive down.

"It's just me," Cam hisses, stepping in and sliding the door closed behind him.

I jump back up as he heads around the side of the desk.

"I can't find the compressed air," I say. "It's usually up here next to her keyboard, isn't it?"

Cam pulls the top drawer open.

"Well, we'll need this," Cam picks up a little key that says *laptop lab* on it. It's the key for the cart. I've seen her use it a thousand times.

"I don't know how I feel about going through all her stuff . . . ," I say, looking at the picture of her and her daughter sitting next to a jar of pens and pencils. They both stare at me.

"Disregard that," Cam says, placing the picture face-down.

I pick it up and put it right back. This is all sorts of badness. But then I remember this is for PingPing. This is for BotBlock. This is for Cam and Izzy and Mama and our futures. And for my promise to Gram.

"All right," I say as Cam goes over to the rolling cart in the corner. I open the next drawer. Nothing but a bunch of extra pencils, pens, paper clips, a few push pins. I close that one and go to the other side. One of the drawers is locked. There's probably no reason to lock up compressed air, so I drop to the next one and try the handle. Bingo. There, sitting among bouncey balls, stickers, cool pens, and erasers, is the can of air. A straw sticking out of the nozzle. Thank god.

I grab it quick, take the laptop from my backpack, open it, and start spraying the keyboard. Dirt flies everywhere. I pinch my mouth closed so it doesn't get on my lips and tongue.

"Which number do you want?" Cam hisses from behind me. I turn real quick and see he is holding the clipboard.

I think numbers six through ten have Bot360, the robot programming software, on them. "Check the front for the program."

Cam scans the front. Mrs. Shareze is very organized with her labels.

"Number six it is," he says, flipping the pencil over.

I hear a squeak at the door. Cam and I both dive low as my heart catapults into my throat. Cam is shielded behind the door of the laptop cart, but he peers around it. I put my finger to my mouth.

"Who is it?" he mouths. I swallow hard. Maybe it's Mrs. Clementine. Maybe it's Mrs. Partridge. And if it is, how the heck are we going to explain this?

I lean down and set the canned air and the laptop gently

on the tile. Then ever so quietly, I place my hands next to them and lean over to look under the desk. The door moves the slightest bit on its hinges, but no one is there. No hands, no faces, no feet. Not from where I can see. I sit up and peer over the top of the desk. Nothing.

"All clear," I say, grabbing the compressed air again.

"Let's do this quick," Cam says, echoing my thought.

I give the laptop one more spray. Hoping it's enough. Then I get up out of the thin layer of dust I've created. I hand Cam number eight and he hands me number six. I double-check the list on the top of the laptop. It says *Microsoft Office, Reading Buddy Solutions, Bot360*.

"Mission accomplished, Mighty Hawk," I say. "Let's fly home." Cam locks the laptop case and we drop the key in the top of the desk. I pull the bottom drawer open and place the compressed air gently inside. Then I kick a couple of clumps of dust and grass away from the desk, so it doesn't look suspicious.

We head toward the door. As we get there, Cam starts to turn left toward the entrance of the building, but I grab the loop at the top of his pack.

"Let's go down the back stairs and out across the playground," I whisper. "Mrs. Ginesh knows we don't do clubs."

We swing right. I'm thinking we're scot-free as I slam the door to the stairwell open.

I stop dead in my tracks. Cam careens into me.

Destin.

He's standing in front of us, blocking the stairwell. A smile slips like a snake across his face.

"What's up, trailer trash? You guys get what you were looking for?" He crosses his arms.

"I don't know what you're talking about," Cam says.

"I'm going to go tell Mrs. Partridge all about your little classroom raid and get you expelled from school."

"No you're not," Cam says, as he comes out around me.

"Don't bother," I say, grabbing his arm. Destin lurches forward and hits Cam in the chest and Cam flies back into the wall. I see his face crinkle up and without even thinking, I grab Destin by the collar and push him.

I don't think about the stairs. I don't think about the tumble to the bottom of the concrete. As he flies back, his foot balances for just a moment, and his arms go out. Three flaps. Then he falls, thumps, clumps down, down, down. And lies still.

Eleven

CAM AND I SIT OUTSIDE PRINCIPAL Partridge's office and I press my hands underneath my thighs, trying to stop them from shaking, but I'm worried the trembling has transferred over to my arms to spite me. *Please don't be dead,* I think.

Mrs. Ginesh looks at me over her glasses like I'm some kind of a crook. It doesn't matter how many times you try to explain it, when one person is at the bottom of the stairs basically looking dead and another person is sitting just fine at the top of the stairs it seems like there's only one scenario. And in that scenario, I'm not coming up roses. I hear the siren come and then go. My legs get restless, like they want to carry me out of here. The principal's office door opens and Mrs. Partridge comes out. I feel my bones getting heavy in my body as she looks at me.

"Please come and take a seat, Lucy."

She holds the door open. I feel as though I'm magnetized to my chair. But I fight the pull and make myself stand. I go in and sit on a chair across from her desk. This one has the same magnet in it. I keep my eyes on the floor, but out of the corner of my eye I see her go around the other side of the desk. I hear her seat click as she sits down in front of me.

"Ehhhrm." She clears her throat and I force my eyes up. Stop looking so guilty, I think. She places her elbows on the table and her fingertips together.

"Destin is at the hospital now. He has a cracked collar-bone, and a very mild concussion."

I can't resist a sigh of relief. I won't be going to jail or anything. At least it sounds like it.

"I swear it was an accident," I say, clasping my hands.

"Nevertheless," Mrs. Partridge says, opening a drawer in her desk and pulling out a file, "I have to put in an inci-dent report and get to the bottom of this. I'd like to hear your side of the story. Then we'll conference with your mother on the best next step."

"My mother?" I ask, my mind flashing to Mama.

"Yes, I put in a call to her a little while ago. She'll be down shortly."

"She will?" I say. "You spoke with her? She said she'd come?" Is the Meditation of Misery over? Maybe she went to see Dr. Vincent and maybe she's feeling better. Then again, maybe she didn't see Dr. Vincent. Maybe she's head in the sand. And that won't be good. Not at all.

"Listen, I-I don't think that Mama is going to be happy about coming over he—"

Mrs. Partridge picks up a mug and holds it between her hands. I can see her scowl over the rim.

"Oh, I'm sure she'll understand," she says, taking a sip.

"I doubt it," I blurt, then buckle my words up tight as she tilts her head and squints at me.

I press my hands underneath my thighs again. How do I explain to Mrs. Partridge that I'm not sure which Mama is coming?

"Maybe I better meet her—" I say, looking over her shoulder at the parking lot. No sign of the old Mustang yet.

Mrs. Partridge raises her hand like she is calming a whole class full of kids. "Is there something you need to tell me, Lucille?" she asks, catching my eyes. She places her mug down. I break the gaze and stare at my knees.

"Is everything okay at home?" She picks up the file in front of her and eyes it from top to bottom, like the answer is going to rise up out of those pages.

I stay silent and a second later she picks up her pen and starts scribbling.

"Everything okay with your mom and dad?" she says.

Dad? I try to stop my nose from making a noise, but it does a little huff anyway. Once I asked Mama what my dad's name was. *Fat Useless,* she said. I wrote it down and went and looked it up in the phone book. Nothing.

"Lucille." Mrs. Partridge waits for an answer.

My mind races. Do I have to tell her all about dads that disappear so well you figure they must be trained magicians? Do I have to tell her about Mama, who's been burying the china in the backyard? Do I have to tell her anything? Are her little notes and scribbles going to ruin my life? Will her scribbles make people come and take

Mama away? I try to get my jaw to calm down, but my teeth are grinding so hard I wonder if they might disintegrate into quarks and leptons. If they send Mama away, we go to foster scare. If we go to foster scare, we're gonna lose our dreams. That's what Gram said. There's nothing *caring* about it. I picture PingPing collecting dust. His pigskin head deflating more, decade by decade, looking alone and scared in the carport, knowing I'm not coming back to him. I watch Mrs. Partridge's pen move across the page. Is she writing a warrant for my future?

"Everything's fine, ma'am," I say.

Her eyes slide up to mine and then down my face to my neck. The bruise from my backpack. I pull the collar of my shirt up so it doesn't show.

"You sure there isn't anything you would like to tell me?" She taps the end of the pen on the desk.

"Not having to do with home," I say. I think I better tell her about the laptop and Destin and the pond quick before everything starts to spin out of control.

Just then the door swings open and we both turn to look.

"I demand a meeting to discuss Desty's trauma!" It's Mrs. Hoffsteader. Mama calls her a pinhead with an inflated ego. Mrs. Hoffsteader breathes in and her nostrils go out as her cheeks suck in.

I turn to Mrs. Partridge. Her shoulders slump the teensiest little bit, but she squares them and says, "Well, you'll have to sit in the waiting area. I'm discussing the situation with Lucille at the moment."

Once my name is out of Mrs. Partridge's mouth I wish it would fly back in. Mrs. Hoffsteader adjusts her jacket and her lips set in a mean line as she walks toward me. She stands just in front of me, but looks over my head and addresses Mrs. Partridge. "Ah, Lucille Peevey. Should have known it was one of *them*."

"You'll really have to wait outside." Mrs. Partridge stands up.

"She threw my son down the stairs and *I'm* the one who has to wait?" Her teeth click together on her last word.

I see Mrs. Partridge's hand begin to shake but she keeps her breathing normal and her words slow down like she's talking to a kindergartener, not a full-grown adult. I don't think Mrs. Hoffsteader likes that one bit.

"First of all, no one threw anyone down the stairs. Secondly, yes, you will have to wait."

Well, that is when Mrs. Hoffsteader just about boils over. And I stand up in case I have to run for it.

"This child is nothing but trouble. Desty tells me she's been bullying him for weeks on end now. You of all people should know the history of her family. They're not well. They're mean and violent." She glares into me and her chin quivers. Who's mean and violent? There's a difference between scared, and mean and violent. I want to stop my voice, but I can't.

"You leave my mama out of this. Your son is the bully. He threw me in the pond just yesterday. Today he slammed Cam into the wall and I pushed him to get him off my friend. He started it!"

"How dare—"

"Enough!" Mrs. Partridge hollers. "Mrs. Hoffsteader, you're leaving my office before I call security. Lucille, you're sitting down in that chair and everyone is going to obey my rules in my school. Is. That. Understood?"

With her final sentence Mrs. Hoffsteader's head is so red, I'm worried it is going to pop off her shoulders. I wish it would. Boom, fly right off her neck and into orbit so I don't have to hear her anymore. Finally, she fixes Mrs. Partridge with a glare. The air settles and Mrs. Hoffsteader hustles out of the room. The door slams and Principal Partridge drops into her chair and takes a deep breath. I start breathing again, too, as I sink into mine.

"Now, where were we—"

The phone rings. She rolls her eyes and picks up the receiver.

"What is it? . . . She said what? . . . Her lawyer?" Her nostrils flare. "All right, I'll be right out."

Mrs. Partridge hangs up the phone and her eyes are kind of shiny. I get to thinking that maybe this would be a good time for me to sneak away.

"I hate to do this, Lucille, but would you mind going back out to sit in the waiting area while I meet with Mrs. Hoffsteader? I promise you I won't take very long and I'll get to you and your side of the story by the end of the workday."

"Okay," I say. But my insides are saying NOT OKAY. Because I have a feeling that Mrs. Hoffsteader is going to brainwash Mrs. Partridge against me.

Still, now isn't the time to disobey any rules, or get further into the muck than I already am. I gulp down my fear and I get up and go to the door. I look at her sideways to see if she's noticing how good I'm being. Hoping I can get some points. When I get back out there, Mrs. Ginesh raises her eyebrows and gives me a can-you-even-believe-this sort of a look. Mrs. Hoffsteader strides past me, looking like a peacock with its feathers out.

"You okay?" Cam whispers as the door slams in my face.

"Yeah, I guess so," I say, glancing through the glass to the parking lot out front. I sit down next to Mrs. Partridge's door and I can hear Mrs. Hoffsteader through the wood. "That girl is dangerous. . . . Surely you . . . entire family . . . dangerous. Delusional . . ."

My stomach tightens like a fist has a hold of all my guts.

"I want her suspended. I want social services to look into . . . situation—"

"We have no grounds . . . social services—"

"She needs to be put into an alternative school."

I think my tear ducts are swelling up so much that I'm getting a headache. One thing is for sure. I'm not dangerous. And I'm trying to form some words in order to express this, but then there's a crash at the main entrance door and standing there in the blaring sun is my mama. And I can tell from the look in her eye that she's not feeling better yet. Not quite. I know just then that this is about to get a whole lot worse. And no one, not even the best scientists, can predict what will happen next.

Twelve

I'M UP OUT OF MY SEAT before she gets to the door. Cam stands up beside me.

"Uh-oh," he says. Cam's been around long enough to know what bad looks like. And this is BAD.

"Mama, Mama?" I whisper, trying to get her eyes down on me. But as she reaches the office, I can see she's drenched in sweat, must have walked down here. Her hair's a little matted in one section, but straight up in another. She's a frayed wire, walking. Her brow is all bent out of shape already and before she even reaches the desk, she's yelling: "Now I'm here and you have to give me my child. She's my child. You can't keep her."

"I'm right here, Mama," I say. Cam's an inch behind me and when I reach back, his hand is there in mine. Mama doesn't hear me. She's got tunnel vision. I see Mrs. Ginesh grab the phone.

"Yes, Trudy, Mrs. Peevey is here. It appears to be . . . urgent." Mama doesn't wait for Mrs. Ginesh to hang up the phone. She heads for the principal's office door. It swings open and Mrs. Hoffsteader is there. She lurches back to stand behind Principal Partridge. Mama waves her hands and points. "How dare you hold my daughter here against her will," she starts. "Your goddamn corrupt system . . ."

I swallow hard as people from track practice start to leave the gym. Their steps slow down. They see my mama. Their eyes go from her to me. Their expressions twist. Half questions, half . . . disgust. The imprint of their wide eyes settles into my mind and fossilizes on my brain.

"We should go," I say, but my words are just a slip of what they were. Nothing of much importance. The kids keep streaming out. I see Jack, Kim, Laura. Snippets of Mama's words trickle to my ears while I glance down at the tiles.

. . . you stupid . . .

. . . don't tell me what I should do with my kid . . .

. . . your sister, she killed him . . .

On the last line I look up, shaking my head. Glimpses of real, glimpses of fiction. They flash together and it's hard to untangle one from the other. The room is too hot.

"Mama," I try again, but she doesn't hear me. She doesn't respond.

"I wanna go," Cam whispers as his fingers tighten around mine. I'm not sure if he's talking to me, or Mrs. Ginesh, or the world.

"Mrs. Peevey, you're going to have to calm down or we'll be forced to call the authorities." Mrs. Partridge's voice has a sense of steel to it now. There's no honey or care from our earlier conversation, and I can tell this episode is enough to make Mrs. Partridge see us just like Destin does. Just like Mrs. Hoffsteader does.

"There are no allies among us," Cam whispers.

. . . you make me . . . sick . . .

Mama picks up a vase from the table and hurls it through the door. I hear the crash. Flinch. Pinch my eyes closed, then open. No matter how you cut it, this isn't a dream.

A breeze comes in through the office window, and I see the sun glancing off the pavement outside.

"Mrs. Ginesh, please call the police," Mrs. Partridge says, her voice shaking.

Not the police, I think. If the police come, everything in front of us changes tracks, just like a train. And I don't want to be a part of it. The air in here is choking me. My space suit is running low on oxygen.

"Cap'n, say the word and we retreat," Cam whispers.

"Affirmative," I say, squeezing his fingers.

We run.

Thirteen

CAM AND I SPRINT DOWN FIELDERS Lane. I hear a set of sirens start up in the distance and I can tell we're not ever leaving today. At least, not together. Not in a direction we wanted to be headed. Not a chance in a million years. Why, why, why couldn't we have luck on our side for once? We round the bend and dash between the trailers. I bolt up the steps and we crash in the front door. Izzy is sitting at the kitchen table and she jumps as we fly inside. She frowns and tears start to roll down her cheeks. I go over to her. Her crown has been cracked in half, and when I get up closer I see a few of the gems are scattered among the newspapers, books, and articles that litter the table. She's tried to make herself a sandwich. The bologna is half in and half out of the bread, and she hasn't eaten a bite of it.

"Hey!" I grab her up, tickling her around the middle, playing like everything is so fun and great. Cam fills up a water glass and slurps it down. I try to calm my breathing, too.

"Sorry, sorry. We got into some trouble at school," I say, hugging Izzy.

She buries her head in my shoulder. "No one was home."

"I know," I say, "but we're here now." I pull back and look her in the eyes. "And we're going to go and play Mission Control, okay?"

Cam places the glass in the sink and heads around me toward the living room. I pick up the sandwich and tuck the bologna inside. As I walk past the phone, I see the voice mail button blinking red.

"You catch up with Cam and I'll meet you there," I say. Izzy grabs on to Cam's hand and heads through the living room door. She stops just before it shuts.

"My crown," she says, pointing to the table.

"We'll have to make you a new one," I say, "a better one." She considers this, seems to warm to the idea, and then goes through the door. I push the voice mail button.

Beep

"Hey, Marge, it's Candace. You missed critique group. Was wondering what's up. Give me a call when you get this. We miss y—"

Beep

"Hi, Lucille and Margaret, this is Dr. Vincent. I received your message and am wondering how you're doing. Margaret, you missed your appointment today. I think I'll stop in to check on you. Give me a call."

Beep

"Hi, Margaret, this is Jean. Wondering if you were

coming in to work today, this week, or, um, at all. Pat isn't happy. Call me."

Beep

"Hi, Margaret, this is Shirley, Shirley Claire from Mental Health Services. I just wanted to check in because we'd received a call from the school. I'm headed over to see you and wanted to know if you want to get a cup of tea or something and chat for a few minutes. Hope you're doing okay. I'll be there in a few."

I lift my shaking finger to the button again. The crisis workers only come out if it's an emergency. I hear a crash from outside and hit the button quickly, ducking over to the window. Mama's running down the driveway. Another crash comes as I see her knock down two trash bins at Mr. Blinks's trailer. Chuck squawks and jumps out of the way of a landslide of garbage. Mama moves like a comet picking up speed. And her target is our trailer. She knocks down bin after bin after bin, like she's making a getaway from invisible predators. I wonder what else happened after we split. I'm wondering what people saw.

I spin back and back and back and back into the living room and then into my room. Out the window. I lift the tarp on the carport and see Izzy sitting in the backseat of the Mustang. She's created a little fort with my duffel and Cam's backpack. Cam has the new laptop out and flips it open.

A slam comes from the front of the trailer. "What's the noise?" Izzy says, covering her ears.

"Uh, nothing to worry about, we're just going to sit here for a few minutes." I pull my school bag from my shoulders and place it in front of PingPing. I look up and Cam and I lock eyes.

"She's back?" he asks.

"Yeah," I say. "Hey, you know . . ." My palms are so wet and I wipe them down my thighs as I look at Cam. "You know, I think some people are coming. If you want to go home, I wouldn't blame you."

Cam rolls his eyes and sneaks two steps toward the front edge of the carport. He slides his hand in between the wall and the tarp and lifts it, and I can see there are some neighbors coming out of their trailers. Great. I wonder if she's gonna start swearing at them out the window, or throwing things from the kitchen, but then I hear a sniffle. And a small voice calls my name.

"Lucy." It's a forced whisper. Scared and sad, and I know how that feels, because that's exactly how I'm feeling right now, too.

"Really, Cam," I say as I duck back toward the window.

"Don't worry about me, Cap'n," he says. "We'll be fine." He jumps into the backseat with Izzy.

"Thank you," I say, my voice coming out much smaller than I mean it to. He only nods. I climb inside the trailer, bounce off my bed, go to the door of my room, and look through the living room.

"Lucy, baby?" Mama's voice filters over the mountains of junk. I pick my way over them and slide the kitchen door open, propping it with a couple books in case Cam needs to communicate. Mama is sitting up against the outside door. The sirens are getting louder and louder. Mama's shoulders start to shake. Mine mirror hers despite my efforts to hold them up.

"They're coming for me, Lucy. They're going take me to Kensington." I see tears start to stream down her face. I go to her. My throat shrinks.

"Don't let them take me. They're going to take me to Kensington. You lose your rights there. You're not human. They'll take my money. They'll take you." At that, both of her hands come up and grab the hair on either side of her head. "They'll lock me up and steal my things, numb my brain."

My stomach turns. Mama went to Kensington before. She called and I remember hearing her shaking voice on the phone, saying that bad stuff was happening. That the nurses beat on the other patients, that people snuck into her room at night, that they would use her money for a dog fight in the basement. Dr. Vincent said these were delusions. Times when reality and fiction blended to make a different story. *Delusional.* A word that people use to describe my mama. I don't like the sound of it. Not at all.

"Don't let them take me, baby girl. Don't let them take me. I'm not going back to Kensington. I'm not going back." She takes a deep breath and lets it out with a sob. "They'll take you and put you in foster care."

Foster scare. Good-bye, Mama. Good-bye, Izzy. Good-bye, Cam. Good-bye, BotBlock. Good-bye, future.

The sirens are loud. I hear the roll of the tires as they pull into Sunnyside. Mama freezes for a moment, then reaches up and slowly, quietly, deadbolts the door. I step back and she slides to her feet.

"They're here!" Cam's head is a dot in the window at the other end of the trailer. He climbs in and rushes to us. "They're here."

"I'm not going. I'm not going. Please don't let them take me," Mama says, grabbing my hands.

My mind is racing.

"I don't want to go, go, go," Mama says, shaking her head.

Go, go, go.

"I don't know . . . ," I say, kind of to myself. But I *do* know. We have two options. Stay and face the police, the mental health people, foster scare. Go and follow our dreams. T-minus zero until liftoff.

I hear footsteps crunch along the kitchen side of the trailer.

"We should go," I say, nodding. "To the coast. We should get out of here."

"Yes," Cam says, rubbing his hands together. "Yes. Let's get out of here."

"Go?" Mama whispers.

"Yes. Go," I say. A thousand steps closer to our dreams.

A thousand steps away from foster scare. A thousand steps from Kensington. A thousand steps from Sunnyside.

A knock comes from the door. I look from Cam to Mama.

"Out the back," I mouth.

Fourteen

"MARGARET? IT'S SHIRLEY CLAIRE WITH THE screeners. Are you home?"

"I'll be right there!" Mama says, then turns to us. "Get what you need quick. Go out your window. I'm right behind you."

"Don't forget your medication," I say, going over to the table. I sift around for her seven-day pill container, but just as my hands are reaching it, she grabs it. I hear the pills bounce and rattle against the plastic as she shoves it into her pocket.

"Right," Mama hisses, grabbing her purse and jacket up off the back of the chair. "Go. Go. Go."

"Margaret, I can hear you're in there." Mrs. Claire's voice gets quieter as I head into my room. Cam jumps up on the window frame.

"Hurry!" I say, heading to the bathroom for our toothbrushes. I couldn't pack those yesterday, on account of good hygiene.

"I just have to grab one thing before we go!" Cam hisses.

"Let your mom know we're going early, so she doesn't worry!"

I hear him laugh as he jumps out.

I grab all three toothbrushes from the side of the sink and push a tube of toothpaste into my pocket. Then I go into our room, pick up the pair of sweat pants I was wearing last night, and pull the keys to the Mustang out of them.

"I'll be right out!" Mama says loudly. I look back toward the kitchen and watch as she pulls a chair over to the door and pushes it under the door handle. Then she opens the fridge. I gulp. Is she looking for that knife? Or food supplies?

"Mama!" I hiss. "No time, let's go!"

She rushes toward me, her jacket thrown over one arm. She grabs a few books off the stacks in the living room, and she has a roll of tinfoil sticking out of her purse. I'm not exactly sure what she's doing with that, but I don't have time to play twenty questions. We climb out the window and into the carport.

We sneak under the tarp. Izzy is sitting there in the blue-green light, looking small. And for a second I think this is bonkers. Then again. The alternative—losing our dreams in foster scare—is worse. I pat her head and go over to the Mission Control station.

"What's going o—"

I put my finger to my lips. "We're going to go on a little adventure."

"Adventure? Like Queen Nomony?" she says.

"Yeah. To a new planet," I say.

Mama comes in through the back of the carport and climbs into the driver's seat. My heart jumps as I hear a rattle and voices from the trailer.

"Hurry, love, they're coming," Mama says.

I wing stuff into the backseat as fast as possible. Junk box, laptop, Mission Control notebook, PingPing.

"What are you bringing that for?" Mama says. "You know we don't have any money for the competition. I've told you a million—"

"I know, Mama," I say, kicking over the crate and pulling the Mission Control fund can from beneath it. "I'm just bringing him to show off and maybe work on."

"What's that?" she asks as I slide into the passenger seat with the paint can between my feet.

"Extra parts," I lie.

"Mrs. Peevey?" I hear Mrs. Claire through my open bedroom window. They're inside the trailer. Mama and I lock eyes.

"Keys?" she hisses.

I push my hand into my pocket and pull out the cluster of keys. Where is Cam? From outside the tarp I hear:

"You little sonofabitch, stay away from my bike." A crash. "C'mere." It's D-Wayne. A second later, Cam is busting through the tarp, wearing a motorcycle helmet. He runs and dives into the backseat.

"Go, GO, GOOOO!" he shouts.

Mom grabs the keys from my hand and jams them into the ignition. The tarp is pulled aside behind us, letting bright sunlight into the murky dark. D-Wayne is silhouetted, but I can still make out his stained tank top and ratty jeans.

"You gonna pay for that!" he shouts as Mrs. Claire and the sheriff come into view through my bedroom window. They begin to climb out and Mama hits the gas. For a second I'm blind. First from the blue flying tarp and crumbling poles, then from the glorious bright sun. When my eyes clear, there's a crowd of people in front of us, scattering like ants in the path of a water hose.

We skid to the side and drive over a tire. Jolting up and down. I grip the top of the door. Rango, Mrs. Barlow's dog, starts barking and I see Chuck run across the road near the top of the driveway. He keeps pace with us for a second. Dinosaur-like legs churning up the dirt. But that rooster, he's too slow to escape, and a second later his legs wind down and stop. He stands staring, right alongside the neighbors. A few of Cam's siblings shout and wave. His younger sister by a year, Mirabelle, seems to be documenting the whole thing with a camera phone. Mr. Blinks smiles and claps, then takes his hat from his head and waves.

We peel out onto the main road and I spot the sheriff and Mrs. Claire running toward their cars. I see D-Wayne's bike crumpled on the ground. As we pass the tree line, Cam, with the helmet on, raises his arms and screams into the sky. Izzy and I join in. PingPing bounces in the middle of the backseat. We hop quickly along the road and I watch the sign for Sunnyside become a dot in the distance. Yeah, we just ran from the law. And, yeah, they'll probably come looking for us. But right now, all I can feel is that we're on our way.

"We have liftoff," I say. I turn in my seat and face the future.

Fifteen

MAMA GOES FAST. FAST AND FRANTIC. Road signs fly past us. Out of Camden, out of Danville, out of St. Johnsbury, through N. Concord and Guildhall. We stick to back roads until there are no sirens to be heard. We must get a little lost because Mama pulls off twice and we find a map in the glove compartment. When the dashboard clock reads 11:30, we pull into a familiar campground.

"Welcome to Pine Acres," Mama says.

The sound of peepers gets louder the farther off the road we get. Mr. Hank, the grampa man who runs Pine Acres, said that they like the dampness of the marsh area just beyond the campground. I try looking for them at night, but I can never see a single one. They're everywhere and they're nowhere. We pass a bunch of RVs and stop in the farthest corner, nestled in the tree line. Normally, we have a tent, but not tonight. Mama gets out and goes to the trunk. Pulls out a couple of blankets, hands me one, and then spreads the blanket out over Izzy and Cam in the backseat.

Izzy is asleep on Cam, and I reach back and shift her to the side, piling a sweater under her head.

She peels her eyes open. "There yet?" she mumbles.

"Not yet," I say, tucking the blanket under her chin.

"Where we going?" Izzy asks.

Mama, who is climbing back into the front seat, pulls out the roll of foil from her purse. "We're going to go live in the country. Whatyathink?"

Cam and I exchange a glance. "No, no, well, not right away," I say. "We're going to go to the coast, remember. To eat shaved ice and watch the stars and, and go to BotBlock."

Mama pulls a hunk of foil off of the roll and takes her journal from her pocket. Nods. Then she starts to make a little book cover out of the foil. I don't know why she's doing this, but she seems to want to protect it from something because she starts saying, "Going to stay one step ahead of the government. They've been trying to get my ideas, but they can't. Not now. My book's almost finished and it's going to make people's minds explode." I watch as she presses the piece of foil flat with her fingernail. I climb into the back with Cam and Izzy. Izzy lays her head on my lap.

"We're going to have a big Colonial-style house," Mama says as she folds. "A small lot near the woods. I'll put you in a good school. We'll have a horse."

"A horse?" Izzy shouts, her eyes popping open, fully awake now.

Where are we going to be getting money for a country house and a horse? That's the real question. But I don't want to bring everyone down, so I just say, "Maybe. We'll see."

Maybe if we win BotBlock. I think it but I don't say it because now is not the time.

"There'll be a long white picket fence," Mama says as she drops the unfinished book cover into her lap for the time it takes to pull out a cigarette and light it, then picks it up and continues to fold and press. "And we'll have ice cream for breakfast. We'll change our names, and go undercover. We'll get a waiver on our taxes."

"What's taxes?" Izzy says.

Mama goes on, ignoring Izzy. "We'll wear the finest clothes and we'll have an orchard out the back, so you can go and pick apples and have apple crisp anytime we want."

"Well, only when apples are in season," Cam says. I nod in agreement.

"Anytime!" Mama says, glaring at him. She looks over at Izzy. "Would you like apple crisp anytime, little one?"

"Always," Izzy says.

"Infinite," Mama says. "And we'll get a nice swing for the new porch." She peels a stray piece of foil off so the edge lines up with the corner of the book, then presses it closed. "Everything we need is right in here." She holds her journal up.

I pull my Mission Control notebook onto my lap, thinking everything we need is in *here,* not in some tinfoil-bound journal. I look at Cam, but he just shrugs.

"Sounds like paradise to me," he says.

"Thatta boy," Mama says, drawing in a breath.

It all sounds nice to me, too. It's a matter of how to get something like that. The real whys and hows of it. People don't just give the Peeveys a big house, a horse, a picket fence, and infinite apple crisp. You gotta earn it. But, yeah, it does sound like paradise and I don't blame a single soul for dreaming it up. Not for a minute.

The breeze pushes the treetops to the side, reaches down and tickles Izzy's hair, takes the smoke and sends it off into the sky. Mama flips the radio on and lets it play at a low volume. I hear the crinkle of her journal as she opens it and starts writing. I yawn thinking what a long, hard day it's been. Cam's snoring lightly on the other side of the backseat. Even PingPing has seemed to slip to the side and is leaning quietly against the door from his spot on the floor. I should really program him. I eye the clock on the dashboard. Midnight. It's officially Friday. I don't have a lot of time. I yawn again and try to keep my eyes open. But it's so warm tucked in next to Izzy. And it's fairly comfortable, too, with my feet propped up on our luggage. I look up at the stars, just to take a quick break before I have to get up and program PingPing. Maybe it's the fact that I've been getting up so early to work on Mission Control, or the fact that I woke up in the middle of the night to go driving, or the fact that it's midnight again now, but either way, my eyes seal up like a ship's airlock, and I'm pushed into dreams.

Sixteen

WHEN I FIRST OPEN MY EYES, the world is a green smudge. I blink once, twice. The birds flitting through the treetops go from having four wings to having two. The pine trees go from fuzzy to firs. The campers morph to their sharp rectangular edges.

Everything bounces back to me. We're in the car at Pine Acres. Cam, me, Izzy, Mama. I scan Cam's and Izzy's sleeping faces. I don't see Mama's head in the front seat. I lurch up, peering over the top of it. She's not there. She's nowhere to be seen.

"Wake up, wake up, wake up," I say, bouncing into the passenger seat. Cam and Izzy rustle to life behind me.

"What's going on?" Cam says, darting to attention. He relaxes when he sees where we are.

"Is it morning?" Izzy says through a yawn.

"Mama's not here," I say, looking around to see if anything is missing that might tell us where she is. We have the Mission Control notebook, PingPing, the can of money. The only thing that isn't here is her journal, her jacket, herself.

I jump out the door and head toward the woods, wondering if maybe she made off into the trees. Would we have heard her go? Just then I hear a door close and spin around. I turn to the little brown building that says WOMEN on one side and MEN on the other. Of course. The bathroom. Mama walks out, wiping her hands with a paper towel. I take a deep breath.

"Didn't know where you were," I say, as she comes up to us.

"Bathroom. That a crime?" Her voice comes out gruff.

I wonder if maybe she didn't get much sleep. "No, it's not a crime. I was worried." I climb back into the car, lean up against the door. Check my watch. Nine a.m. I flip to the countdown, even though I already know what it's going to say. The numbers don't lie. T-minus twenty-four hours until competition.

"It's getting late," I say to Cam.

"I couldn't agree more," Mama says. "We need to pay and get out of here." She hands me a credit card and nods toward the administration building. "Should be open by now."

"I'll power up the laptop," Cam says.

I nod, sending him a silent thank-you.

"I have to pee," Izzy says. Mama places the credit card in my hand and gets back out of the car.

"Everybody do your business and let's get going," she says. She and Izzy make their way across the lawn. Cam looks like he is considering it and heads toward the bathrooms, too. I tuck the card into my pocket and follow, seeing as we're going to be on the road first thing. I pee as quick as I can and then rush to wash my hands. Mama is at the sink helping Izzy wash hers and she mutters, "We better hurry up so we can get out of here."

I don't need her to tell me twice. I run as fast as I can out the door of the bathroom to the administration building.

"I'm hungry," Izzy calls behind me, opening the bathroom door with a creak.

I turn and do a skip-step backward. "I'll see what I can find."

I go in through the swinging door and see the counter's filled with convenience store treats. Reese's Pieces, Twizzlers, PayDays. My stomach reminds me of missing dinner last night. I pick up a PayDay. Peanuts have lots of protein in them. I also pick two bags of regular Doritos and one bag of sour cream and onion for Cam. A little TV buzzes above the counter. The screen is on but the volume has been turned way down.

Green Mountain Weather: 75 degrees and sunny, it says in the corner as a well-dressed weatherman walks around in front of a map. Underneath, the checkout area is empty. Hank is nowhere to be seen. I spot a little bell with a note attached to the front of it. *Ring for assistance.*

I cross the wood floor and hover my hand over the bell, only I don't ring it. I don't ring it 'cause as I glance back up at the weatherman, a little banner is flying across the bottom of the TV screen. The banner is covering the weatherman's feet, and it reads: *AMBER Alert: New England: Kidnapping suspect flees police with three children. Suspect considered dangerous. News at 9.* My stomach almost spits up the emptiness inside of it. Is it us? I gotta tell Mama. I drop the candy and chips on the counter and turn toward the door.

"Welcome to Pine Acres, how can I help you?"

I whirl around. Hank drops a newspaper next to the chips and his face breaks into a smile. "Well, I'll be. I recognize that face. Lucy, isn't it?"

I put on a genuine smile. Hank is nice. He has short white hair and his scarecrow shoulders hold up a pair of rainbow suspenders attached to some paint-splattered pants.

"Nice to see you, Hank!" I say, coming back over to the counter. He leans up against it, resting on his arms.

"I wondered who was rumbling around in the middle of the night."

"Just us," I say, trying not to look at the TV. I'm happy to see him, no joke, but all of a sudden I wonder if my face is breaking out in hives with the effort it's taking to look normal.

He lifts a coffee mug toward me like he's cheersing and takes a sip. "Must be headed on to that program you guys go to. What is it again?"

"Robo—" I slam my mouth shut, realizing maybe I shouldn't be telling everyone where we're going. Sure Mr.

Hank is a friend, but you just never know, now that we have the law on our tail. "Roboville. It's a town in Massachusetts. Next to Boston."

Mr. Hank swallows the coffee and looks at me sideways. "Really?"

"Anyway, we got in sort of late and I wanted to pay for the night." I lift the card and drop it onto the counter in front of him. Then I move my shaking hand out of view fast.

"All righty then, super." He nods his head and picks the card up. If he notices that I'm all shook up, he isn't showing it.

"Well, that'll be ten dollars for one night. You have plans to stay through tonight as well?"

"No, Mr. Hank. Thank you," I say, clasping my hands behind my back.

"One night and the candy and chips?"

"That would be good," I say.

As he leans down to count the items I glance up at the TV. *Channel 3 News,* it says across the screen then pans to an anchor lady.

"That'll be nineteen ninety-five." Mr. Hank swipes the card and then pulls a small paper bag from next to the cash register. He places the card on the counter and flicks the bag open. Then he puts the items in one at a time.

"How's your mama doing these days?" he says.

"Pretty great," I say. He curls the top of the bag shut and turns to the credit card machine. "Our dial-up is slow," he says, tapping a small screen. "Some things don't change." He whistles and looks up at the TV. My mouth goes dry as it says *AMBER Alert: New England* across the screen. The camera zooms in on the anchor lady, who looks pretty serious about whatever she's reporting. Please don't let it be us, I pray. The screen flashes to some blurry footage of our carport tumbling. Great. Stupid Mirabelle. I'm almost 100 percent sure that this is her iPhone video. I scan Mr. Hank's face, wondering if he can decipher the picture. The Mustang is half hidden by the tarp.

"What's this all about?" he says, reaching over for the remote under the window. I don't know if I should jump across the counter and tackle him? Let him pick it up? Flick it out of his hand? Fake a faint? Right when he is about to grab it, the credit card machine spits out a receipt. His eyes flick to that and he pulls the receipt off, adjusting his glasses to see it. I exhale as quiet as I can.

"Well, I'll be damned," he says. "Darn thing didn't go through."

I swallow hard as the broadcast goes on above his head. It flashes to a picture of my mama. *Margaret Peevey* it says across the bottom. I'm in a spaceship spinning out of control. Everything is feeling jostled.

"I guess I'll give a call," Hank says and picks up the phone.

"No!" I shout. The phone spills out of his hand and clatters on the counter. He looks up at me like a startled deer.

"What's the matter?" he says.

"Just—" I say. My world starts spinning, orbiting around my head faster and faster. How can I explain this? I back toward the door, getting ready to make a run for it.

"Well, the card isn't going through. Unless you have another I'll have to call the company and see why it's being declined."

All of a sudden I can breathe again, but not for long. His eyes scan me and he cocks his head to one side. "Is something up, Lucy? What's going on? You worried?"

Act normal, for crying out loud, Lucille. I step toward him, not back.

"No, sorry, Mr. Hank, nothing's up." I slap my hand over my forearm. "I yelled 'cause I, uh, I think I got a bee sting is all. Nothing's up." I go right up to the counter so my chin is just over the high top. "I can grab another card from Mama, or uh, or get some cash from her." I hold out my hand, but keep my other pressed onto my forearm like I'm covering up a sting. I look at his face, hoping to heck he's buying it.

Mr. Hank looks around the room. "I didn't see a bee in here. Let me see. Do you need some ice?"

"No, no, we Peeveys are tough," I say, taking the card off the counter.

His face softens and he smiles. "I know you are. You go get another card or cash from your mama and I'll find you something to cool off that bee sting, nevertheless."

I gulp and keep my hand clasped over my arm.

"Yes, sir," I say, going over to the door. "I'll be right back. Thank you."

I push the door open and the spring squeaks and then slams behind me. My heart is pounding so hard that I can't hear the birdcalls all the way back to the car. We're in trouble. That's what I'm gonna tell Mama. But when I get back to the spot where our car was—there's no one to tell. It's gone.

Seventeen

I'VE LOST MY SHIP OUT IN space. I swallow real hard and scan the trees. All I see are branches and birds and sharp mosaic pieces of blue sky mixed in with pine needles and bark. I step back toward the office building, my eyes filling with tears. Why would they just take off like that? Cam and I have a strict leave-no-man-behind policy. I look around the side of an RV and then head over to another one and look on the other side of that, too. Nothing. I stand still and make myself take a few deep breaths because I feel like I have an alien in my throat. It's flopping all around, trying to poke its way out.

"*Psssst.*"

I start and look around one side of the RV that's right in front of me

"*PSSSST,* up here, Cap'n."

I look up wondering why Cam would be on the top of an RV, but nothing is there. Instead, I see his face staring at me through a tiny back window.

"What are you doing in there?" I say, rising up on my tippy toes to get a better view.

"Hurry, get in," he says. The RV starts with a *thrumm-*

mmm, and I run to the door. I pull it open. All our stuff is jammed in behind the driver's seat. Bags, bins, PingPing, motorcycle helmet. Everything.

"We get invited to breakfast or something?" I ask, latching the door behind me. I climb the steps. "Where's the Mustang?"

Cam comes out of the back. "Sshhhhh," he says. I feel the RV switch into gear and we roll forward slightly. Just then I hear a clatter. I look out the window and a lady and a man are running toward us, heading away from a faucet on the side of the bathroom. Plates, pots, and pans skitter along the ground behind them.

"What's happening?" I ask, grabbing Cam's shoulder.

"Come back here!" the lady shouts, reaching her arm out like she is going to pull the RV back somehow.

"Are we stealing this?" I ask as we lurch out of the campground and onto the main road. I see Mr. Hank come jogging out of the building. He and I lock eyes and his head cocks to one side. Mr. Hank is about to connect all the dots, but before he does, the campground disappears behind the curtain of pines running the length of the road. I turn toward the front and pull aside a sheet that separates the cab from the rest of the RV. Mama's in the driver's seat and Izzy is buckled into the passenger seat.

"Get in the back and sit down!" Mama shouts.

I close the curtain for a minute and sit down at the little table. My head is filling with sparks and I try to blink them away. Cam sits down across from me.

"What's going on? I thought we were doing good?" I think of Mama last night with the infinite apple crisp and the dreams and the sky.

"When you went into the cabin, we turned the radio on," Cam says. "Seems like it's all over the news. They're playing it off like I was kidnapped. Like your mama's dangerous. They ID'd the Mustang. She flipped."

Mama seems to be driving really fast. I hang on to the edge of the table and try to stay focused on what Cam is saying.

"A minute later, we saw these two people leave their RV, saying something about having a broken water pump and needing to do the dishes."

That's why they had all the pots and pans. "Oh god," I say, shaking my head.

"So next thing you know, your mama tells us to haul everything in here and hide. Izzy and I did . . . while your mama drove the Mustang somewhere."

"You got the Mission Control fund?" I whisper, getting up onto the seat to look over the back of it. PingPing, duffel bag, junk bin.

"It's there," Cam says. "I got it myself." He gets up and comes over. My heart clanks a beat on my chest, 'cause I'm not seeing it as I push PingPing to the side and pick up the backpack, looking for the metal tin. Cam reaches down and lifts up the duffel bag. There it is. I collapse into the seat.

"Anyway," Cam says as he goes back to the other side

of the table, "she couldn't have taken the Mustang very far, because she was back in a few minutes."

We lurch along the road. I watch as we pass a pasture. White and brown horses dot the green field.

"Horsies! Look, Mama!" I hear Izzy say through the sheet.

"Goddamn, goddamnit, sending in the cavalry," Mama says. "Sending in the goddamned cavalry."

"Horsies?" Izzy says again, this time it's a question.

"Metaphorically, metaphorically," Mama says. "Bad news."

Bad news is correct. I drum my fingers on the table and think. I gotta reason with her. I gotta do something. I gotta get up and *do* something. This is all wrong. We're stealing someone's RV.

"This is more trouble than we would have been in originally," I hiss at Cam. We jolt over a bump and Cam slides across the seat, planting his foot at the last minute. He stays propped up sideways. A picture takes a nosedive off of the wall, glances off my arm. I grab it just before it hits the floor.

"Uh—yeah, we're in it pretty deep," Cam says, pushing himself back up. I look down at the picture in my hand. It's that couple. I barely recognize 'em 'cause in the picture they look so happy. Not scared. Not upset. Not what we made them. Just happy.

"Uhhhhh." I flip the picture over so it's facedown on the seat next to me. "This is *chaos*."

"Well, chaos *is* exciting," Cam says, "if nothing else."

"We need to focus, Cam," I say. "We got a goal here. Don't forget our goal."

"Right."

"We're supposed to get to BotBlock, not go to jail," I say, running a hand through my hair.

"Yeah, I know. And we're going to."

We turn and Cam and I look out the window. We slide onto a paved road and everything smooths out. We stop bouncing around like bobbleheads. The remaining picture on the wall stops shaking like there's an earthquake. I take a deep breath and place my hands on the table. Push myself up. I go to the curtain that separates the cab from the rest of the RV and pull it open.

"Mama, we need to turn back," I say, teetering as she swerves to avoid something. I can't see what it is from my spot. I wait until we're back in the center of the lines. "This is wrong. We need to turn back."

"What?" Mama spits. "We can't go back there. Have you lost your mind? They're after us, Lucille, they're after us and they know what the Mustang looks like. I told you they were after us. I've been trying to tell everyone."

I grip the curtain tightly as we zoom down a road past a farm and then a soccer field where a bunch of kids run from one end to the other. Izzy sits up in her seat and looks out at them.

"You think the world's kinder than it is," Mama says.

"Stay down, Izzy." She reaches over and presses Izzy's shoulder down. Izzy sinks back into the seat.

"Better safe than sorry," Mama says as she hits the button on the radio. I watch her hand shake as she flips from news to music to news.

And coming to you next is news of a kidnapping out of Vermont yesterday—

Topping the charts in 1960 was this classic from the—

Keep your eyes peeled for a 1980 Mustang, red, chipped paint with a dented door on the driver's side—

"Just a small town girl,
livin' in a lonely world,
she took the midnight train goin' anywhere—"

I sink to the floor between the two seats and listen.

AMBER Alert . . . Camrin McKinney was among the three children in the car. Both girls are believed to be biological—

Mama slams the radio off.

My stomach feels queasy. "Now you see?" Mama says. "We can't go back. We have to get away."

Away where? I scan the scenery, not recognizing the route we usually take. "Are we headed toward the coast?"

"I know where we're going, Lucille. Go sit in the back with Cam and let me take care. The world's crazier than you know."

My jaw feels tight from grinding my teeth. I want to tell Mama that *she's* crazier than she knows, not the world. But I can't. I can't think of a reason to turn around. I can't think of a reason to stop. We're in trouble. We're *really* in trouble. And we're on the run. She's right about that.

"Let's work on Mission Control," Cam says from behind me. "It'll keep our minds busy."

"Right, go play," Mama says.

I cringe at the word *play*. Clench my fists. "It's not—"

"Not today. Not yesterday," Mama says, shaking her head, not hearing me. I push up from the spot in the middle of the floor and make my way to the table. Try to make myself comfortable. But it's like there is something starting to churn and roll in my stomach. Something I have to push down. And I do. I take a seat and look around the RV. Nice white curtains stand out against dark red walls. The table has a marble pattern to it. I trace the patterns with my finger. The cushion on the seat is plastic-y, but really comfortable. There is a long, couch-like seat running along the wall behind the passenger seat. I pick the picture up from its spot next to me and place it back on a little plastic hook on the wall. I stare at the faces and think, *sorry,* at them. I make sure the picture is straight and then gaze out the window.

"This doesn't look familiar at all," I moan. "I don't think we're going in the right direction."

Cam digs into the bags behind me and then comes around and places our Mission Control notebook and laptop on the table. Then he flips to page 7 and turns it toward me. My dream page.

"I already know what it looks like," I say, pushing it away.

"Maybe you need a reminder," he says.

I groan and take the Mission Control notebook.

There's a picture of Sunnyside. I drew it a year ago, but it looks so babyish to me now. The trailer park has a dark storm cloud over it. There is a car, the Mustang. It's shiny and new, not all busted up like it is now, and it's blazing out of there, driving way far away. You can tell it's far because of the stars coming out of the tail pipe and the lines showing the speed. Out in front of the car is a beautiful house and a dog, and a little pot of gold next to a tree. There's a picture of Gram up in the sky, looking down through a window, smiling over the new house.

"We got the beginning right," Cam says. "Blasting off!" He pretends like he is grabbing on to a wheel, speeding into the future.

"Yeah, that part's right." I take a deep breath. I pick at the pages with my thumb. "Maybe we can return the RV as soon as we get into Seahook?"

"Yeah, we could make that happen. Anything's possible."

I flip the pages to our Mission Control Protocol for Optimum Achievement and scan the list.

"Well, we swapped out the laptop," I say, pulling the pencil from the spiral binding. I drag the pencil through the line item. Then scan the rest of the list. I scan it a second time, wishing it would change before my eyes. We haven't finished anything else.

"We're in trouble, Cam. We haven't programmed Ping-Ping, we don't even have enough registration money for the competition." I drop the pencil on the page.

"Hold up!" Cam says. "I forgot!" He stands and tucks his hands in his pockets. He's smiling real big and I'm wondering what the heck he has to be cheery about. He pulls his hands out and rains a cluster of crumpled bills across the table.

"You didn't," I breathe, thinking of D-Wayne running after him yesterday.

"He wanted to make a donation," Cam says.

I pick up a bill and press it flat, then another and press that flat, too. We count up twenty-five dollars.

"How did you . . ."

"I told you. I'm much faster than him. No one catches Mighty Hawk," Cam says, doing a little dance. "We have enough, right? Put it with the fund."

"It's more than enough to cover the rest of the registration," I say, not believing. Cam goes around the seat and pulls out our paint can filled with cash. I check the curtain to make sure Mama isn't seeing our money stash. Cam grabs a screwdriver from the junk bin and pops the lid. I hand him the money and he puts it in and reseals it. Then tucks it back behind the seat.

I cross out *Save up registration money*. Two items down, three to go. I check my watch, 10:00 a.m.

"T-minus twenty-three hours until competition."

Cam hands me the laptop and grabs PingPing. "We got this. Let's program ourselves a robot!"

Eighteen

I LOOK OVER THE PROGRAM SPECS. "It looks like he'll need to go fifteen meters and then turn left. I think that's about three bursts, so you want GoForward, GoForward, GoForward." I point to an icon and Cam drags it into the BotProg window.

"Zzzzcrshhhhh," Cam says as he drops the icon into the program.

I think Cam's decided it's not exciting enough for him without sound effects.

"Zzzzzzcrshhhhhh," Cam says as he drops another icon. He adds the third with a final "kapploowww." I wait for him to finish.

"Then we need a soft right." I point to the screen and Cam grabs an icon with the mouse. "I think you've got the wrong one," I say. "If you hover over it a description will pop up. Here." I reach over his shoulder and hover over the correct icon. *SoftRight* it says in a little pop-up box. I pick it up and drag it.

"Incoming," Cam says. "Zzzzzzzcrshhhhhh."

I release it into the BotProg window. I pull the claw command over next.

Every once in a while I look up, hoping I see the sign for Seahook, New Hampshire. Or a sight-seeing sign that might point us toward the ocean. But nothing. The truth is, I didn't know there were so many dirt roads in the whole USA, but it seems that if you want to stay off the radar, you can just drive from one dirt road to the next to the next, avoiding the pavement. I watch the signs slide by and try to recognize some of them. Burk's Dairy, Al's Fish Hatchery, Old Mountain Road, Old Bridge, and Old Creek. Southwest to Bristol, Laconia, Franklin.

"Does Laconia sound familiar to you?" I ask Cam as I watch pine trees and rocks slide by the window.

"Yeah, I think so," Cam says. "I think it's in New Hampshire."

"Right," I say. "You're right. It's up north, though, and we seem to be north of it . . ."

"But it's still in New Hampshire, and you know what else is in New Hampshire?" he says, getting up and pulling PingPing toward the table.

"BotBlock," I answer, going to our supplies. I pull up my duffel bag, take out the MCIIB, and set it on the table.

"Destiny," Cam says, tapping his knuckles on the Mission Control notebook.

"I'm hungry," Izzy says from the front seat.

I picture that lost PayDay and my stomach makes a loud growl.

"I'm hungry, too," Cam says, looking toward the back of the RV.

I follow his gaze, wondering what kind of snacks these people might keep.

"Reconnaissance mission?"

Cam nods.

"I'm really hungry," Izzy says, getting her whining voice on. "I'm really, really hungry."

"Enough," Mama grunts.

"I'm really—" Izzy says. Then she switches into her Queen Nomony voice. "I demand a banquet."

"Just a minute," I say. "We'll see what we can find."

"Mama?" Izzy says.

"Izzy, *I'll* help you in a second," I say.

"Mama, are you okay?" Izzy says as the RV lurches to the side. I spin and run to the curtain, pulling it open. I see Mama mutter to herself and then she takes a ragged breath in. The kind that you take when you're trying to keep cool. The kind you take when you have fireworks going off in your brain, when you think your heart might explode.

"Can you stop the R—" but before I can finish my sentence, Mama slams the brake to the floor. And it's not because I said so. I topple forward into the empty spot between the seats, my forehead barely missing the radio console. Everything grinds to a halt. I see Cam land on the floor between the seats. He's got PingPing in his hands. And good thing, because it looks like that robot was about to crash down the stairs. The Mission Control notebook teeters on the edge of the table, then plummets to the floor. I lift myself to a sitting position. Izzy unbuckles her seat belt. When I look up, Mama is sitting there, jaw dropped. Dust floats in the partially open window next to her. Then, as if someone flips a switch, she starts to scream.

Nineteen

"I COULDN'T STOP ON TIME. HE came out of nowhere!" Mama screams. Her hands wave and then crumple into fists as she starts hitting the steering wheel.

"Did we hit someone?" I lift myself up and look out the window. My blood roars through my veins as everything jumps into hyperspeed.

Mama brings her hand over her mouth and starts crying.

I slide past Izzy's legs and open the passenger-side door, jumping down to the ground. My heart slams against my chest as I run to the front of the RV. Cam is right behind me.

"You stay right here," I hear him say to Izzy. "Don't move."

I slide across the dirt road and look at the bumper. Is it some kid? Is it a dog? Was it a biker?

Nothing is there. I lean over, check in the shadows beneath the RV. Cam and I are shoulder to shoulder, looking all around. I stare off into the trees, wondering if what we hit may have wandered. But nothing. As I come full circle I see Mama through the windshield. I look at her face. It can't be nothing. Not with the fear in her eyes. A terror so real I can feel it from here. I look again. There has got to be something there. But all I see is empty air, all I smell is pine trees, and all I hear is birdsong.

Mama grasps the door handle and falls out of the driver's seat.

"Do you see anything?" Cam whispers.

"No. There's nothing here." I scan the Park and Sit across the road. Just a picnic table and parking spots.

Mama runs to the front. Covers her mouth with her hand and screams again.

"Shhhh, shhh, shhh," I say, going toward her as she drops to her knees. Her hands up by her head.

"Mama," I say. Afraid she is way out beyond me. "What is it?"

She looks up at me. "I think he was already dead. Did you see the bugs? He must have already been dead."

Chills climb up my spine and Cam comes in closer.

"Do you think we're dealing with ghosts?" he whispers. I slap his arm.

"I highly doubt i—"

"Oh, Robert, oh, Robert. Oh. Oh." Mama covers her mouth again and crawls backward. "Do you see him or not, do you see him?"

My tongue is stuck still and Cam and I exchange a look. He shrugs. I don't know what to say. I don't see anything. I follow Mama's gaze, but the spot where it lands is empty. I manage to shake my head just slightly.

"I need to get some help. I need some help." She closes her eyes hard and teardrops fall out of the sides of them.

I go to her. Kneel in front of her. "Mama. Let's get back in the RV."

"He looked so yellow," Mama says. "Jesus, did you see how yellow?"

I reach toward her, and as I do she pulls away from me, like my hand has teeth in it. "Oh god, no. Doesn't make sense," she says. Scrambling up. She presses against the front of the RV.

The air around us feels like it's filled with electricity. I wouldn't be surprised if my hair is standing straight up on end. I swallow. "Maybe—"

"Not you, too." She looks at Cam's hand. Grabbing it and flipping it over, turning it to examine his wrist.

"Mrs. Peeve—" he starts, but then she drops his hand and runs into the camper. I follow her up the steps. She rushes into the back.

"No, no, no. 1874 to 1963, 1874 to 1963. It's not real." She slams a cupboard open and then another and finally comes up with a bottle that has some brown liquid in it. She drinks it like lemonade, but that's not what it is. I can tell from the shape of the bottle that it's not lemonade at all. She sucks it down her throat. It's empty before the second gulp. She drops it into the sink. I blink once. Twice. I don't know how to make this better. It's like she's having a nightmare, but she's awake.

I grab her purse from its spot on the floor. "Did you take your—"

"Move out of my way," she says as she storms past me, down the steps, and toward the woods.

"Mama, where are you going?" I ask, dropping the strap and following her.

She stops when she gets to the picnic table. She places both her palms flat down on the table and takes three long breaths. But she's shaking from head to toe like there's a thunderstorm under her skin. She sits down and slumps onto the table, closes her eyes. Her head quivers just slightly.

"She won't move, not for a while," I say. I hear Cam and Izzy talking on the other side of the RV. Cam helps her down and they come over to the Park and Sit. As soon as they see Mama crumpled on the picnic table, they both mirror her. Cam's mouth slides into a frown, matches my own, matches Izzy's eyes and shoulders.

"Do we have a protocol for this one?" Cam pulls the notebook from under his arm.

I reach over and press the pages closed. "No one has a protocol for this one."

I hear Izzy sniffle next to me and I open up my arm like a wing, and wonder what we're going to do now.

Twenty

"We gotta move the camper," Cam whispers. "Can you drive it off the road?"

"I can try." I unlatch Izzy from my side. "Can I see that notebook?"

Cam hands it to me. I hold it out to Izzy. "Queen Nomony," I say with my best Captain Juniper Ray voice. "We have a Vintage Carrier problem and need to conduct maintenance. I need you to review the plans and design new ones for the next phase." I watch her eye the notebook, hoping she'll bite. She doesn't use her queen Nomony voice, but she does wipe her eyes and take the book from me.

"Keep an eye on the mother ship, too," I say, looking at Mama.

Izzy nods and I hope turning this into a game makes it a little bit better. Dr. Vincent calls it a coping mechanism. I'm not sure it's really working, but Izzy sits down at the end of the table, opens the notebook, and pulls the pencil from the side.

"All right, let's move this camper," I say. I wipe my hands and notice they're shaking badly. I jump in the driver's side and climb in, pulling the door closed behind me.

Cam goes around and gets into the passenger seat. I pull my seat forward.

"It's just like driving the Mustang," I say out loud to help convince myself, "but a whole lot bigger." I push my feet down to put the brake pedal to the floor, but my foot swings into empty air.

"Crap."

"What?"

"My foot doesn't reach the pedals." I try again, but again my foot swipes through air. I scooch down, but as it is, I can barely see over the steering wheel.

"This is a nightmare," I say, sitting back up. "This is a real nightmare."

I see Izzy jump off the picnic table and come over. She waves.

"What is it?" I stick my head out.

"I think there's a car coming!" she says, waving toward the back of the RV. My hands tighten on the steering wheel and my eyes find the sideview mirror. I hear a rumble off in the distance.

Worse than a nightmare. "We gotta move now. If they stop—if they put two and two together—we're in trouble."

My mouth feels like it's filled with moondust. I run my tongue over the insides of my cheeks but nothing helps.

"Maybe, uh." Cam snaps his fingers over and over like that will help him think faster. "Maybe . . ."

"Maybe?" I say. "Maybe?!" I squeeze the steering wheel.

Cam takes a deep breath. Closes his eyes. Then exhales

very slowly. His eyes flutter open. "I can do the pedals?"

"Ohhh." I don't like the sound of that, but I don't think we have any other choice. "All right, let's do it. We better go now."

Cam scrambles to me. I wedge my feet over to the side and he climbs in wheelbarrow style to work the pedals.

"What do I do?" he shouts.

"Press the brake in!" I brace myself against the seat and grab the key in the ignition.

"Right. Cap'n, locked and loaded!" Cam shouts.

"Starting engine!" I press the key away from me. The key chain jingles on Cam's shoulders as he adjusts his position below them. The engine roars to life. I check my hands. Ten o'clock and two o'clock. Then I check the sideview mirror. There's a definitely a car and it's coming in hot.

"All right, now take your hand slowly off the brake."

I feel Cam shift to the left, pushing against my leg. I try to make room for him, but the RV jerks forward hard. "SLOWLY!" I shout. I turn the wheel to the left and aim for the tire tracks that are traced in the dust next to the picnic tables.

"All right, press very slowly onto the gas," I say.

"Affirmative," Cam mutters and the RV lurches off the road, toward the trees. I spin the wheel a little to the right to straighten it out.

"Brake, brake, brake!" I shout as we sail past the picnic table. We slam to a halt and I hit the steering wheel, but recover just in time to push the gearshift into park. I take a deep breath. The dust filters up around the windshield. The music in the oncoming car gets louder and louder.

"Let's go!" I throw the door open and jump out. Cam crawls out behind me and we plant ourselves around Mama like fence posts.

"Act natural," Cam says. The car crests the hill and sails past us, music thumping, windows open. A cloud of dust billows out behind it as it passes, and I take a deep, sandy breath.

"That was close, Cap'n," Cam says, licking his lips. "I mean, nothing we couldn't handle, of course."

"Right," I say as I look over at Izzy. "We did it. Thanks for the warning, Queen Nomony."

She gives me a halfhearted smile. A fly flits around Mama's head, and I wave it away. Izzy comes and climbs onto my lap and shows me the picture that she has drawn. Big house, white picket fence, a tree that looks more like a flagpole with antlers on it. A pile of apples.

I glance over at Mama. The only movement I can detect is her jaw working. I glance from her to the notebook to the RV and I wonder if anything in our Mission Control book will ever have a chance of coming true. I look up at the sky, wishing Gram's face were there telling me what exactly we should do now.

Twenty-One

CAM PUFFS HIS CHEEKS OUT AND I wonder if, even for someone who loves action, this is too much. Out here, unknown territory. Astronauts stranded on Mars. Cam gets up and starts wandering around the picnic tables. Occasionally jumping up onto a bench and then back down.

"Uh, Mama?" I say real quiet. She shakes her head and doesn't look at me. Her eyes flick around under her eyelids. A car comes rolling by and my heart plummets into my jeans. This is bad news, but then it keeps on rolling. I glance at its taillights as it heads down the road.

"Maybe we should get back into the RV," I say, thinking it's always safer under cover.

Mama shakes her head.

"We *are* running from the law, after all," Cam says, picking up a few pine needles from a tabletop. He releases them, watching them spin to the ground.

"Yeah, less people around, less people noticing us." I check the road for another car.

"I'm hungry," Izzy says, jumping off of the bench.

I ignore her and keep looking at Mama. She seems like

she is fighting to open her eyes. Finally she pulls her lids apart and nods. She gets up real fast and hurries over to the RV. I follow her in the door and up the steps.

"You should probably take your medication," I say as we get up the stairs. I pick up her purse from the pile of upturned belongings behind the passenger seat, but before I get a good handle on it, Mama turns on me. As soon as she does, her face is telling me that she is trying not to lose her temper.

"Leave it alone. Leave me alone," she says, grabbing the strap. It comes free of the pile and whips toward her; the paint can with our BotBlock fund gets caught and tips hard onto its side. I watch as the lid comes loose and lands flat, the ball of cash rolling to the edge. I kick it back in and try to block the opening with my foot. She just turns and heads to the back of the RV. She goes past the kitchenette and into the tiny room, slamming the door behind her.

"Do you think she noticed it?" I ask, pulling the can up.

Cam shakes his head. "I don't think she noticed anything," he says.

"You're probably right." I push the lid onto the can and wedge it far into the shadows between my duffel bag and Cam's bag.

"I'm really, really hungry." Izzy's climbing onto the seat now.

"Okay," I say, thinking it would be good for all of us to get something into our bellies. "Reconnaissance mission."

I head to the back of the RV.

"While you're doing that, I'm going to try and figure out where we are," Cam says, sliding past Izzy. "I saw a GPS while we were trying to get the car off the road."

"Good thinking," I say as I open a cupboard above the sink.

Izzy settles at the table with a huff as I work my way from top to bottom opening and closing doors. Glasses, dishes. Cereal, Ramen noodles. Forks, spoons, knives. They nearly blind me with their sparkle. I pull out the trash bin. Even the trash smells like lavender.

"Houston," I say quietly, "we are on another planet." I reach to the right and open a cupboard. Jackpot. Canned chili, beans, vegetables. They're all on these racks that keep them held into the shelf. I pull one can out and hold it up so I can see the lettering. Big Mama's Gourmet Organic Black Bean Chili. No Market Basket ninety-nine-cent junk. This is the real deal. I put it up on the counter, thinking that it will make a heck of a lunch. I open the fridge, too. There are cans of Diet Coke lined up in the back and in a little drawer near the front there are all sorts of cheeses. They say havarti and smoked gouda and Vermont Cabot cheddar and Tipperary cheddar. I run my fingers across the green label that circles the "Tipperary." For a second I imagine standing out in front of the cheese case at the store, trying to figure out which cheeses would be the best to buy. Those are the choices I'd like to be stuck with. Not "When should we run away." Not "What should I say to Mama when she looks like this." Not "How are we going to keep away from the cops" or "How are we going to make it to BotBlock." But "What type of fancy cheese am I gonna buy today." What type of creamy delicious cheese am I gonna to try? Maybe this one, maybe this one, maybe all of them. I'll have that, and that, and that! How much does this one cost? Oh, who cares? That's nothing! I'll take the whole case.

That's exactly the kind of choice I want to make.

I pull out the Vermont Cabot cheddar. People talk about Vermont Cabot cheddar all the time. If we get cheese, it's the orange kind. Velveeta. Good, but not real. I pull the wrapping back and then slide the silverware drawer open. I slice a big hunk of it off the top and split it into three pieces. I drop the knife into the sink and go over to the dining room table. I hand a piece of cheese to Izzy.

"Queen Nomony, we've got a specimen, here." She rolls her eyes but takes the cheese. "It appears to be some sort of organic material. Believed to be native food."

She bites into it and then takes another bite before swallowing the first. I go up to the front and hand Cam a couple of pieces of cheese. He has the key half turned in the ignition.

"Do you know how to run this?" I ask, seeing the digital map in the console.

Cam nods, examining it. "Richie Frank had one that we used when we carpooled to away games."

Richie Frank's name is actually Dan. He just happens to be rich, too, so Cam and I have always called him Richie.

"Okay." I take a bite of the cheese as I make my way back to the kitchenette. It's smooth, sharp, and creamy. A burst of flavor that lingers on my tongue.

"What was the last town we went through?" Cam says.

I can't remember any of the names except for one a long time ago. "We passed Laconia about forty-five minutes ago," I say.

"Okay. If I could just zoom out," Cam mutters. I hear a *blip-blip-blip* as he tries different buttons.

I pull the tab on the top of the chili can and then dig around for a pot. I empty the chili into it. It hits the bottom of the pan with a loud *schluuup* sound. I put it onto the stovetop and flick the knob to high. Then I get a spoon out of the drawer and stir.

It's getting dark and I hear the patter of rain, which has taken up residence on the roof. Otherwise, it's mostly quiet here in the back of the RV. Spooky, tummy-churning quiet. Over the simmer, the only other sound I can hear is Mama softly whispering and crying in the back room. And despite the other noises, it fills my ears. I watch the chili swirl and the beans separate from one another, and I wonder if it's like going into space. If you go out far enough, you don't ever come back, not even if you want to. Is it worth not going to foster scare for this?

My ninth birthday was the one I realized the truth about moon shells. It started out nice. We spent the day walking the beach. Mama didn't seem happy, but she didn't seem angry either, and Gram was there, too. We got ice cream and shaved ice. Then we walked the beach and stumbled upon the Bot-Block competition. I was chasing Izzy over a sand dune and once I reached the top, three robots with caterpillar bases rolled toward us, then turned as they crested the hill and headed between a set of flags, going back the way they'd come. I watched them until they disappeared into little dots in the distance. When I pointed them out to Gram, we headed over to the green at the center of town to see what was going on. Turns out a lot. There were tons of kids. Robots were battling in every corner. On the beach they were racing each other. Some were going alone through a roped-off obstacle course.

Mama sat down off to the side to write while we had sausages with peppers on top from a vendor in the food tent. After that, we headed back to the hotel. I was getting excited to stay up till midnight. And since we were at the beach I was expecting midnight singing and dancing in the sand, just like last year. But when we got into the hotel, Gram started getting Izzy all ready for bed, and Mama just lay down.

"You want popcorn, Mama?" I asked, grabbing the remote from its spot next to the television.

"No, thanks," Mama said quietly. I bounced on the end of the bed.

"Starbursts?" I said, not getting why she was feeling so blue on such a bright day. I squirmed up the bed and gave her a squeeze around her shoulders.

"No, thanks," she said again. When I leaned over to look at her, she didn't meet my eyes. She was looking out past me.

Almost like she was in the middle of a daydream. A real sad one.

I got up and flipped the TV on and pulled Star Wars Episode IV: A New Hope *from my bag and put it into the DVD player. I watched it but that didn't even get me to ten thirty, so I put in the* The Empire Strikes Back. *Izzy snugged into Gram's side and fell right to sleep. Gram gave me a wink.*

"Why don't you grab my purse right there and you can go on down to the vending machine and get yourself a few snacks?"

I shook my head. I was too into the movie, and anyway, I would be having cupcakes soon.

As the clock reached 11:40, I looked over at Mama. She was staring out at the moon and the stars, but not in a way that made me think she wanted to go out there. Gram must have seen me look over at her.

"I'll bring you down to the beach, baby girl," she said. Gram got up and picked up Izzy. Izzy was just three then, and she would sleep through anything. Gram started tucking her into the stroller.

"What's wrong with Mama?" I asked, getting my sneakers.

"She just had a bad week," Gram said. "She needs to sleep. Maybe she'll feel better tomorrow." The way Gram said "maybe" made me think that maybe *that wasn't true.*

I Velcroed up my shoes and followed her gaze again. "Maybe she just needs some moon shells," I said.

"What's that?" Gram said.

"Moon shells. They suck up the moonlight at night. They have magic in them."

Gram tucked the blanket around Izzy. "Well, let's go get some, then," she said.

We went out to the beach and we kicked the waves, but Gram didn't make the wave-smashing sound. And Gram didn't bring a birthday surprise. And actually, Gram didn't bring any poetry to say at the stars. Izzy woke up halfway through and started bawling and I was feeling more tired than usual. I pulled a few moon shells from the shore and tucked them in my pockets.

"We can go back, now," I told Gram as she tried to shush Izzy.

We made our way inside and I ran into the hotel room and around the edge of the bed. "I got you moon shells, Mama," I said, uncurling her fingers and pressing one into her hand. Her fingers moved and touched the smooth surface on the inside of the shell, and for a minute she stopped staring out into space and locked eyes with me.

"Thank you," she whispered, taking my fingers. She bent them and kissed my knuckles. Right then, I thought the moon shells had cured her. But later that night, I woke up to her sniffling and crying. The week after that, she went to Kensington and Gram came to Sunnyside. The week after that, I realized that moon shells were just hocus-pocus.

"Moon shells have lots of magic," Gram had said. "But Mama needs more than magic. She needs a plan. The hospital will help her make a—"

"I think we're in northern New Hampshire!" Cam hollers.

Just as the room filters back to life in front of me I notice a thick line of smoke rising from the pan.

"Crap!" I shout and toss the smoking pan quickly into the sink. I hit the tap, but nothing comes out. Of course, broken water pump. I forgot. I turn the faucet to the off position, waving at the burned mess.

Cam comes over. "Not goin' so good?"

"I just got to thinking," I say. I grab a towel and wipe the chili off my thumb.

"I can help," Cam says. I appreciate Cam trying to be a hero of sorts, even if it is just about making lunch.

"We're in the land of plenty." He shrugs. "We'll open another one."

"Thanks," I say. "I'll—I'm going to go and check on Mama."

Cam nods and presses the can opener to a new can of chili. I pull the block of cheese back out and cut a bunch of slices, spreading them out on a plate. I also find a sleeve of Club crackers and put them in the middle. I bring the tray over to Izzy first and she pulls three off. Then I head to the door in the back.

"You need any help?" I ask as I pass Cam.

He looks at me with a smirk and pulls a dish towel off the mini-fridge handle. "Cap'n, I've been cooking myself lunch since I was four. Hate to brag."

"Right," I say, tabling the plate on one palm. I open the door to the bunk very slowly and step into the yawning darkness.

Twenty-Two

"'I HAVE BEEN ONE,'" MAMA SAYS.

I lean down next to her, but she doesn't turn to me. She's curled up facing the opposite wall.

"Mama?" I reach out to touch her arm with my free hand. She jumps like I put a poker to her back instead of my fingers. I jump, too, holding the plate against my stomach so the crackers don't slide off.

"It's just me. It's just Lucy. I wanted to make sure you're okay," I say.

"I'm okay. We'll be okay. We'll be fine," Mama says. She sounds drunk, but sometimes she sounds like that even without drinking. Gram said it has something to do with brain chemicals. I wonder if that small amount of alcohol would be enough to make her drunk.

"I wanted to see if you want some lunch," I say. "We're making some chili. I have some crackers and cheese here."

I reach my hand out to feel for a light switch.

"What?" Mama says. I hear the sheets rustle slightly as she shifts.

"You haven't eaten in a while," I say. "Want some cheese and crackers?"

"No, no, 'I have walked out in rain and back in rain . . .'"

I sit down on the floor, recognizing that poem. Same one she was reading when we went out for the midnight ride the other night. "Mama, can you listen to me for a minute? I don't know if we should've done this. We should've brought you to Kensington. This isn't any good anymore." The rain beats the rooftop.

Mama shakes her head. "Don't send me there. Not with them. I told you I don't want to go with them. I told you, I didn't want to go back there. It's not safe." Mama barely breathes between sentences. "They're after us, anyway. They're coming for us. We have to hide and stay inside. High. Like, like balancing on a pin in the sky."

She flips toward me and I see her face is rough and wet from tears. I take the opportunity to hold the plate of cheese and crackers out to her.

"Please eat something. You're not listening," I say, wondering what balancing on a pin in the sky is supposed to mean.

"We're not going there," Mama says. "Promise you won't bring me to Kensington. Promise me, okay?"

My voice is strangled because I don't know who's going to help her if Kensington can't. But she seems so scared. I don't know what to do. I wish more than anything that Gram was here.

"Mama, you saw something earlier, what did you see?" I ask. I want her to tell me it was a bird. Maybe a bird

149

swooped into the window and it's no big deal and we can just keep on going as soon as we all have a rest.

She cries and covers her mouth with her hand. "Oh god, Rob," she says, flipping back to the other side. Her shoulders shake.

"Rob?"

"'I have been one acquainted with the night.' 1874 to 1963." Her fingers work along the edge of the blanket.

"Robert Frost?" I say, wondering what that is like, to have someone who is inside your head all the time just pop out into the street. One second in and the next second out.

She cries louder now.

"You saw Robert Frost?" I say.

"Leavemealoneleavemealoneleavemealone," Mama says, covering her ears. "He's dead. 1874 to 1963."

A shiver goes up my spine. "I think we better get you to Kensington."

"No, promise me, promise me, promise."

"Mama, you're sick." My palms feel sweaty along the bottom of the plate.

With that Mama flips over and before I can blink, the plate of crackers goes flying out of my hand.

"I said I'm not going there!" Mama yells as the crackers and cheese come down on my hands and hair, bouncing off my shoulders and onto the floor. I try to catch the plate, but it teeters, slamming against my cheek, then dive-bombs into my lap. Mama pulls the blanket up to her neck.

"'I have been one . . .'"

I'm frozen with my hands in the air. My cheek throbs.

"Mama?"

Nothing.

"Mama?" I say again.

"Leavemealoneleavemealone."

I unfreeze my arms, reach for the plate, and feel around for the crackers. They're everywhere. I push them onto the tray as quick as I can. But it's not quick enough and I can't find all the stupid pieces and—

"Why?" I shout.

Why does she have to make it so hard? I slam the last crackers onto the tray and then I think, *What the hell am I doing?* Why do I have to clean up this goddamned mess? I catch a cracker that slides down off my shoulder and yank the door open. I pass Cam, who lifts the spoon out of the pan to look at me. Pass Izzy, who reaches out to me. I run and fall down the steps and smash through the door. Into the rain. Nothing makes sense and nothing is the way it should be. Mission Control is out of control. Way out. Farther out than we've ever been. Plans are supposed to work. Promises are supposed to be kept. I look up at the sky and rain falls down, falls heavy into my eyes, and I throw the crackers onto the ground and stomp on them until they're teeny tiny crumbs. I destroy them under my feet. I raise my head, wishing the raindrops would thunder down, do me a favor, fill up my lungs. But they don't. So I scream into the trees.

I scream as long and loud as I can.

Twenty-Three

I COLLAPSE, EXHAUSTED, SOPPING WET AT the small dining room table. Cam pulls out a bowl and puts some chili in it. Izzy sits quietly next to me, staring at the picture in her book. But she doesn't color or draw. She looks like a tiny mouse. A tiny little frightened mouse. Cam pulls the back door open and looks in toward Mama.

"You want something to eat, Mrs. Peevey?" he asks. But she doesn't respond and a second later he walks back into the kitchenette. He picks up the pan and brings it over to the little dining room table, places it in the middle, and sets down three spoons. He hands one to each of us. I set mine on the table. My stomach twists, thinking of Mama back there. A miserable bag of bones.

"You have to eat something," Cam says, picking up my spoon and pressing it into my hand.

I hold it and spin it. Izzy takes no time to dig her spoon in and pull out a gigantic mouthful. She chews and swallows.

"Good?" Cam asks, taking a big scoop.

"Real good," Izzy says around a cheekful. She holds her spoon in her fist and shoves it back into the pan.

I put my spoon in, too, trying to push the frenzy out of my head. Lift the spoon and take a bite of the chili. It warms my mouth, my throat. It's good and smooth. It's not metallic like the kind we get sometimes. The kind that sort of tastes like a can.

"What are you thinking about?" Cam says. "What happened?"

"It's good. The chili. It's real good," I say, not wanting to talk about it.

Cam rests his spoon on the table, then goes over to the fridge and opens it, pulling out a soda.

"But really? What are you actually thinking about?" he asks as he takes three glasses from the shelf and pours the soda into the cups, giving Izzy a few sips less than us. He hands one to me. I take a sip, feeling the fizz bounce around my mouth. I start to feel the teensiest bit better.

"She saw Robert Frost," I explain.

Cam raises his spoon, then lowers it.

"I mean, when we stopped. I think she saw a dead Robert Frost. She's sicker than I thought." I take another spoonful of chili. But no matter how much chili goes in, no matter how much the soda makes everything clearer, I can't figure out what step makes sense to take next.

"I think we have to turn around," I say, trying it out loud to see if it makes sense. I drop my spoon. It clanks against the edge of the pan.

I watch Cam as his chewing slows. He swallows and puts his spoon down.

"Mama's worse off," I say before he can jump in. "We should have sent her to Kensington." My voice seals up on the words.

"She doesn't want to go to Kensington," Cam says. "She said it herself."

"I know," I say, "but they can help her there. I mean, that's what they do."

Izzy scoops the last of the chili from the edge of the pan. Cam picks it up and goes toward the kitchenette. He's shaking his head just a little bit, but I can see it.

"But what about PingPing and the BotBlock—" he starts.

"We'll go next year," I say, hating the thought, trying not to look over at PingPing.

"Don't you think it was hard enough to get out of Sunnyside once? It took us a year to get up the registration money. It took us a year to collect all the parts for Ping-Ping. Then destiny itself puts us on the road to Seahook and . . . and we're going to bail?" Cam says, dropping the pan into the sink. I groan. I press my hands over my eyes.

"Why is everyone against me," I say, getting up.

"I'm not against you," he says real quiet. He shifts his feet. "It's just, you're the one who thought this whole thing up."

"Excuse me?" I say.

"Not in a bad way. I mean, taking control of our futures. Thinking of big plans. Maybe if we alter our path"—Cam comes around the kitchenette and picks up the Mission

Control notebook, flipping through—"make some minor changes, like getting your mama to the hospital first?"

I flop onto the couch. "Are you crazy? You really think we'd be able to drop Mama at a hospital and continue on to BotBlock? Did you hear the news?"

"Well, not that exactly. But I'm sure we can do anything we—"

I wave his words out of the air. I know exactly what he is going to say. "Cam, no. I don't want to hear your 'we can do anything' speech right now. Okay?"

"We—"

"Okay?" I say, making it real clear.

"Forget it," he says. He slides past me and pushes the curtain open, then slides it shut and I hear him sit down in the front seat.

"It's impractical," I say to the curtain. Totally impractical.

Izzy looks up at me over the edge of her glass of soda. I run my hand through my hair. I just want to go away. Go away from this place just like I wanted to go away from Sunnyside. It doesn't matter where we go, nothing seems easy.

Izzy comes and scoots in next to me. I don't open my arms up to her. All I want is for Mama to do this. For Mama to be a mama. To sit up and come out here and drive us to BotBlock and be normal. NORMAL. To Izzy and to me. Imagine how easy it would be. Just go there and put the robot in the competition. Izzy gets up and picks the notebook up from its spot on the table. She sits next to me and inches it into my hands. She presses the spiral binding against my fingers over and over. I groan and take it. Then she goes and lays her head down on a little pillow at the other end of the sofa. Sally Ride stares out at me with determination in her eyes and I look away. I look toward the floor, then the ceiling, anything but at her face. Finally, I can't take it and I flip the notebook open. But then there's the design plans for PingPing staring out at me. I flip the page again, and then there's Cam's YMCA ticket to a better life. I flip again and see the apples and the house and the white picket fence. I slam the book closed and flip it to the blank back cover.

I look at the mess all around me. I'll clean up, take my mind off things. I pick the laptop up off of the seat where it landed. Then I lift the MCIIB from the seat next to it. I unzip it and check the transmitter to make sure it isn't banged up from the wild ride. It looks fine, so I slide it back in. A little gold-edged frame sticks out. I sigh. Pull it out. Look straight into Gram's eyes. I wonder which is the right way to go. Gram smiles out at me, unanswering. I look from one end of the RV to the other. Suspended in a small spacecraft, waffling among the stars with a busted navigator and a bruised-up copilot. Carrying heavy cargo. It seems to me I've made a promise bound for breaking.

Twenty-Four

THE CURTAIN SWINGS OPEN. I GROAN. What now?

"Cap'n, this is Mighty Hawk."

"No," I say, and tuck my mouth back into my elbow.

"Are you afraid, Cap'n?" Cam says. I turn and see him hanging on to the curtain, leaning in the other direction. What the heck does he think he is doing? His chest is all puffed out and he is looking real serious. He goes over to the pile of junk and picks up the motorcycle helmet. He pushes it onto his head.

"Cap'n?" he says, sliding the visor open so I can see his face.

"No." I sigh. "I am not afraid."

"And if we were to be taken down by a laser-beam firing squad, would you be afraid?" He comes over to stand in front of me and gives a sharp salute.

"Cam, I'm not afraid. And I know what you're doing, and it's not going to work. Not this time."

"Cap'n." Cam drops his arms to his waist, so both his fists land on his hips. "All you need is a pep talk. I didn't realize it before. But you've stopped believing."

"It's not that," I say. "It's that I realized some basic facts—"

"Now, hear me out, Cap'n." He waves a hand. "It's not that you stopped believing in *the mission*."

I look sideways at the Mission Control notebook.

"You stopped believing in your decisions."

My stomach starts to squirm. I wish he would quit it with this already.

"You stopped believing in the logic of our situation and you stopped believing in yourself."

"Enough," I say. This is one of his most overdramatic speeches of all time, and he's actually pretty prone to them. I lie down on the couch, shoving my feet toward Izzy's shoulders, and turn toward the wall so we're head to toe. But Cam doesn't get the hint, apparently, 'cause he just keeps on going.

"She begged us not to let them take her," Cam says. "She begged us. I was there. You saw the look in her eyes."

I shove my face in farther, wishing the fabric would go around my ears.

"Is that true, Cap'n?"

Why, why, why.

"Well"—I hear him start pacing the length of the trailer—"did she or did she not ask us not to let them take her?"

"It's true," I say, flipping over. "But—"

"No buts!" he says. He turns sharply and struts toward the back. Then turns and comes my way again. I sit up.

"It's true," he says. "And do you think she would be happier in a hospital bed than that bed?"

I swallow hard, looking at the door in the back. Thinking of how many complaints she had about Kensington. "No. Maybe. I don't know," I say. The delusions got so bad. "Probably not."

"I accept we've run into some obstacles." Cam holds his hands out. "Theft for example." Mr. and Mrs. RV stare at me from their spot on the wall. I look away from their smiling faces.

"But that's to be expected," Cam says.

"Is it, though?" I say.

Cam comes through in his real voice. "Yeah, it is." He sits down across from me, leans in. "The truth is, your mama was already running. We just made it easier."

"I don't know." I get up and go to the table. Sit down across from Cam. I take the Mission Control notebook and spin it, see how many turns it can go before it lands still. "That's just it. We've messed so much up that even if we get to BotBlock, it doesn't fix anything. Not anymore. Not really."

Cam stops the notebook in its tracks and pulls the motorcycle helmet off his head. He tucks it into the seat next to him. "I know. But it would be a sunny spot, something to hold on to. Something to build the future with. Otherwise, what? We bring your mom to a place that she hates. We send you and Izzy to strangers. We send me home to D-Wayne. We have nothing, Lucy."

159

I press my hand onto the Mission Control notebook.

"But say we did win . . ." I feel the dream wrap around me like a warm blanket. "We would have enough to get your gym fund started. We would have enough to get Mama some help and we would both have scholarships to college."

"That's what I mean," Cam says. "That's the stuff that makes it bearable."

That's the stuff that puts you in control of your future. I want to press my believing into the pages, and will our dreams out into the world.

"Well, Mama isn't going to drive," I say. "Another obstacle."

"She might not drive," Cam says. He leans forward and talks really quiet. "But you can."

"Cam. We can't drive this RV in tandem all the way from here to Seahoo—"

"It's not that far," Cam says, gesturing toward the front. "The GPS pinpointed us in northern New Hampshire, in a place called Wolfeboro."

Wolfeboro, I haven't heard of it. "How far is that?"

"I'd say about sixty miles," Cam says.

Sixty miles. "That's not quite the same as pulling into the Park and Sit."

Cam's eyes light up. "Yeah, but, uh, there's this girl I know that is crazy good at building things."

"Building? What am I going to build?" I say. "A space-ship?"

He gets up and goes around to our stash behind the driver's seat. "I don't know," he says, as he digs around. Finally, he stands up and brings the junk bin and sets it down at the table. "You're the brains of the operation."

"Ugh." I scan the materials. "What good are these going to be?" I pick up a piece of wood and roll it off my fingers. It clunks back into the bin.

"I don't know." He reaches in and picks up a handful of wires. "But whatever you decide, Cap'n, I'll be your wing-man." I push a piece of metal to the side and pull up a different block, a chunky piece of wood. I press it between my hands. Maybe.

"All right." I nod. "All right, maybe. But let's make sure we're all set with everything for BotBlock first. We only have one chance."

"Right," Cam says. "Our moment."

I press my watch. Three thirty p.m. "T-minus seventeen hours."

"Plenty of time to test a robot and drive sixty miles. Plenty. Of. Time." Cam winks. I just shake my head.

"Not with our luck."

Twenty-Five

I WAIT UNTIL THE RAIN LETS up for a few minutes and hurry outside. I set PingPing down on the ground and the laptop on the picnic table. I look over the program commands that we have put into our BotProg window:

```
Start
GoForward
GoForward
GoForward
SoftRight
SoftRight
GoForward
S3Trig
S4Trig
GoForward
XDelay
S4Retract
S3Retract
SoftLeft
GoForward
```

```
GoForward
GoForward
EndProg
```

It looks about right. I pull the program into the BotRun window and pick up my MCIIB. I pull out the transmitter. The Sharpie flies out with it and lands on the ground underneath the picnic table. I pick it up and as I'm rising I realize I should put PingPing's name on his belly. That way when we win, everyone will know the name of our superior droid. I uncap the Sharpie and use my neatest handwriting to write *PingPing200* around the barrel. Then I put the Sharpie away, uncap the transmitter, and insert it into the USB port on the side of the laptop. Let's hope this works. I lean down and flip PingPing on.

Wuw-whir, wuw-whir. His elbows and claws twitch with life. His eyes flick on and beam across the Park and Sit. I take a look at the dark sky and silently beg it not to rain for the next five minutes.

"Let's hope this works, buddy," I say. I take the remote control from its spot around PingPing's neck and make sure it's turned off so I'm not mixing signals. Then I take a deep breath, slide the mouse over to the go button, and click. PingPing rolls forward in three long bursts.

"C'mon," I say as he jolts to the right twice. He moves forward again. So far, so good. Then he stops, his elbows drop, his fingers open. He slides forward.

"Pause," I say.

Delay works. Then fingers close. In the rescue mission, this will be around a flag.

"Now retract." I watch as his elbows close. One soft left—he executes perfectly. Then he moves forward in three bursts. Ideally, he'll have the flag and be over the finish line. If all our calculations are right. If not, he'll be smashing up against a wall somewhere. I flip the Mission Control book open and look at the details. We'll have three practice chances on the course before running the race, so if I have to change the distance forward it shouldn't be a big deal.

I close the BotRun program and eject the transmitter, then pick up the remote control and run PingPing back to me manually. *Pling-tink, pling-tink, pling-tink,* he says as he rolls my way. The lights on the metal detector light up. I stop. Toggle back. *Pling-ting, pling-tink, pling-tink,* he says again. I release the joystick and go over to him. Pick him up and set him down next to me. I look down where he was standing. A penny. I reach down to pick it up but freeze when a clatter comes from the RV window. I look up to see Cam's worried face. He slides the window open.

"Is it heads or tails?" he says. "Because if it's tails, you leave that penny right where it is. We don't need any extra bad luck in here right now."

"Don't be silly," I say, but when I look down, I take a big sigh of relief seeing it's heads. Of course, I don't believe in that fake superstition, but if there's ever a time we could use a lucky heads-up penny, now is it.

"We're safe," I say, picking it up.

"Great," Cam says.

I tuck the penny into my pocket, then pick PingPing up with one hand and the laptop up with the other. I climb the stairs.

"How we doing in here?" I say.

Izzy is sitting at the dining table winding three pieces of wire together. Cam has a few pieces of wood, some springs, and wires in front of him.

"Well, I'm making a new crown," Izzy says as she threads a green wire over a red one.

"Good idea," I say, setting PingPing down behind her.

"And I pulled out everything I think you might need for a foot extension," Cam says, gesturing over the tools. "What do you think? You can use something here, right?"

I scan the blocks of wood and select a sturdy three-quarter-inch piece. I place it up against the sole of my shoe. It's about the right size. I grab a green spring and test the tension against the top of the table. It barely gives. Cam selects another block of wood and hands it to me. I put it at the other end of the spring.

"If we can sandwich the spring in the middle and then secure the top piece of wood to my foot . . ."

"Then we might have something," Cam says.

I grab a thick-gauge wire from the bin and start

securing the top piece of wood onto the spring. Cam puts the extra pieces back into the bin.

"This is too long," Izzy says, holding up her crown. The white wire extends past the red and green. Cam grabs the wire cutters and gives it a snip.

"Thanks," Izzy says, lifting it and shaping it to her head. She pulls it off and tries to work the ends around each other. Cam helps her get them connected while I put the bottom piece of wood on. Then I grab another piece of wire and I secure the contraption to my foot by running the wire across the top of my shoe.

I shake my foot. It's a little floppy, so I get another piece to secure around my ankle.

Izzy places the crown on her head.

"That looks pretty good, Queen Nomony."

"What's that for?" she asks, pointing to my foot.

"It's going to help take us out of here." She nods like she understands.

"You ready, Cap'n?" Cam says, setting the box of junk parts behind the driver's seat.

"Two seconds. Let me make sure Mama's really not feeling good enough to drive. Then we'll go, okay?"

Cam nods and I hop to the back of the RV and open the door.

Twenty-Six

"HEY, MAMA, ARE YOU OKAY?" I say real quiet, squinting into the shadows.

"I'll be fine. I'll be fine," she mutters.

"We're going to keep going to the coast, okay? Do you want to drive?"

Mama's voice is strained like she's been crying since I left this room a few hours ago.

"Don't you see we've gone from poetry to Poe? I don't want to do anything."

My throat squeezes. "All right, well . . ."

Her voice gets rough. Gets louder. "You're not bringing me to Kensington, are you? You're not taking me there."

"No, we're not. We're going to Seahook and that's all. Nothing to worry about," I say. Of course, there are a million things to worry about, but I'm not about to bring them up now.

"Fine, fine," Mama says, and I think that's all I'm going to get out of her, so I turn back toward the interior of the camper and close the door. I look at Cam, who is leaning up against the passenger seat, the curtain standing out just behind him as if it were a cape. He's holding his motorcycle helmet under one arm. Izzy stands next to him, sporting her new wire crown.

I take a deep breath and check my watch. It's ticking toward 9:00 p.m. "T-minus twelve hours until competition," I say, heading for the front.

"T-minus twelve hours until we begin our new life," Cam says.

T-minus twelve hours until promises are kept or broken, I think. My new shoe flips and flaps as I head past the curtain. A few fat drops of rain thud onto the windshield. *Of course,* I think, but I don't pay it any mind because there is nothing I can do about it, anyway.

"C'mon up, Izzy. Bring a pillow," I say as I slide into the driver's seat. I press my foot into the brake and feel the pressure through the sole of my shoe.

"If we take it real slow," I say, touching the gas just a teensy bit.

Cam climbs into the passenger seat and Izzy settles on the floor in between us. She shoves her thumb in her mouth.

"You need to get as much rest as you can for tomorrow," I say, watching her eyes flutter open and closed.

I press the brake in, take a deep breath, and turn the key. The console lights up, casting the whole interior in green. "Vintage Carrier has power," I say, breathing out.

The GPS map floods the cabin with a blue tint. Cam hits a few buttons. "Setting navigation," he says.

I hit a lever on the right side of the steering wheel. The windshield wipers peel the layer of rain from the glass.

"State." A British accent comes out of the speaker.

Cam starts punching letters. *N-E-W*.

"You know how to spell Hampshire?" he asks, but before I can say anything it fills the word in for him.

"City," the British lady says next.

"That's Seahook," I say. "S-E-A-H—"

Cam punches the buttons as I spell the word. Again, the computer completes the thought.

"Street."

What street is the pavilion on?

"Queen Nomony?" I say. She pulls her thumb out and sits up.

"Yes, Cap'n?"

"Could you grab me the Mission Control notebook?"

"Yes, sir," she says, ducking out of sight. I secure my seat belt. I hear her shuffling around in the back. She returns and hands me the notebook. I flip to the flyer in the front and scan the print.

"Oh, right. Ocean Avenue," I say. "I should've remembered that."

Cam starts typing and once again the British lady finishes.

"What number?" Cam asks.

"Fifteen," I tell him.

He punches it in and the GPS springs to life. "Acquiring

satellites, it says." Then a new map blinks and holds steady on the screen. I examine it. *Arrival time: 10:30 p.m.*

It's 9:00 p.m. If we go straight without any problems it will take us an hour and a half.

"That seems like a long way to go with a fake foot," I say. I squeeze the steering wheel, trying to think what Gram would say.

Cam shrugs. "Taking it slow, and factoring in potential problems, ETA will be midnight. Registration opens at nine a.m. tomorrow morning. We have lots of time."

"Right," I say. "We have plenty of time."

Still, Cam is not the one in the pilot seat here.

"Can you make it keep us off highways?" I say.

Cam switches into *Tools* and selects *Preferences*. Then hits *Avoid Highways*.

The map acquires satellites again. I press my block foot into the brake.

"With new coordinates, we'll still be in by midnight, Cap'n," Cam says.

"Great," I say.

Izzy starts to settle back into the spot between the seat. "Queen Nomony?" I say. She sits back up, giving me a queenie glare.

"What now?" she asks.

"Could you get the picture of Gram? I'm pretty sure I left it on the table."

Izzy's brow unfurrows. She must think this is a worthy

errand to be sent on because she gets up and a second later ducks back between us, holding Gram out to me.

I take the picture in my hand, wondering if she would approve of what we're about to do. Breaking about a million laws and running through the dark night in an RV that isn't ours. Nope, this isn't how Gram would do it, but somehow, I think she'd understand. I tuck the picture in the spot next to the speedometer. It props up just fine on that little ledge at the back of the steering wheel.

Cam makes a crackling sound.

"Captain Juniper Ray, commencing launch checklist now."

"Commence," I say, shifting in my seat.

"Seat adjustment?" Cam says.

I reach down to the left and pull the lever up, tilting forward slightly. I move it a bit back and a little forward until I'm comfortable.

"Check," I say, releasing the lever.

"Mirrors, right and left?" Cam says.

I look to the mirrors on each side, locate the little buttons on the door, and adjust them until I can see the road behind me.

"Check," I say.

"Ignition," Cam says.

"Check," I say, resting my hand on the key. "Ignition already initiated."

"Navigational coordinates acquired and ready to go,"

Cam says, tapping the *Go* on the touch screen of the GPS.

"Captain and techs, in position and secured?" I say.

He pulls his seat belt around, clipping it in on the other side. "Secured and ready. It's your ship, Cap'n."

Hands at ten and two, I hear Gram saying. *You stay in control.*

I take a deep breath and gaze into the dark night. I place my foot carefully on the brake pedal and draw down the lever on the right of the steering wheel until the little arrow at the base lands on D. Then I lift my foot lightly off the brake and move it over to the gas, pressing down until the dirt below us squeaks, and we pull around a loop and out onto the road again. The camper jostles from left to right as I steady it in the right lane.

I chance a quick look at Cam. He gives a thumbs-up. "And that's a star-spangled takeoff for flight 220. Next stop, BotBlock."

Twenty-Seven

THE NIGHT GETS ENDLESSLY DARK AS we pass from sleepy town to sleepy town. And I hear Gram in my head, telling me, *Eyes peeled, head calm and clear.* I try to make it so. Soon Izzy's light snores float up between Cam and me. I take a quick glance down. She's holding a pillow like it's a teddy bear and sucks her thumb quietly. I don't hear a sound from Mama. I hope she's drifted to sleep, too. Sometimes, sleeping can really help your brain. That's what Gram used to say.

As we wind down the road, I keep my eyes on that yellow line. I keep the RV going below thirty miles per hour. Cam flips the visor down and a little yellow glow beams on him. He opens the Mission Control notebook. I look over and see he's on our Mission Control Protocol for Optimum Achievement page.

"Two: Complete, practice, and program PingPing200," Cam says.

"Well, we finished. It may need some alterations, but we did finish it, so that's technically done."

I hear the pencil scrape across the paper.

"We have three test runs. We'll make any adjustments we need," I say.

"Right," Cam says.

"Take a right in two hundred feet," the British lady says. I breathe out and move my foot from the gas to the brake. I press in once, twice, three times, then turn the wheel onto Vineyard Avenue. Once we're straightened out on that road, Cam says, "Item three: Go to BotBlock (and win)."

I hear the pencil meet the paper.

"Don't get ahead of yourself," I tell him.

"Too late, I crossed it out," Cam says. "I'm feeling confident. Four: Make dreams come true. That one we'll have to wait on. Good progress, though."

I squeeze the steering wheel, liking the sound of his words. As the rain slicks the window, I can see Gram in the periphery, like she is here along with me. As we wind our way along a river, in between mountains, then down into flatter terrain, I start to recognize where I am, and memories of previous trips to the coast rush back to me.

My tenth birthday. Izzy was four and wanted to stay up late like me. Mama told her she could, but she whispered in my ear, "She'll be far into dreams by ten, trust me."

She actually made it to 11:00, but I watched her eyes drooping for half an hour before she actually let them close.

I counted the minutes until 11:49.

"Shall we make our way to the beach?" Mama said, pull-

ing up the surprise bag. I eyed the shape at the bottom of it, wondering what she got me this year. I bounced off the bed and grabbed hold of my sneakers, slipped them on. Out of the corner of my eye, I saw Gram dig around in her big purse.

"Can you carry this along?" Gram asked Mama. Mama went over with the surprise duffel and they started shuffling things around. I tried peeking to see what they had, but they were pretty good at being sneaky. Once everything was adjusted, Mama picked Izzy up and put her into the carriage and we walked out into the night.

We didn't run down to the beach, but we did get into the sand and I took my shoes off and smashed the waves. Gram pushed Izzy along, singing a little melody, and Mama sat down in the sand with the bag. She opened it up and I sat down across from her, knowing how this worked.

"First from me," she said, pulling up a rectangular gift. I took it from her and peeled away the wrapping paper. The Collected Works of Robert Frost. I rubbed the front and held the book to my heart, knowing how much Robert Frost meant to Mama.

"Thank you," I said. She smiled from ear to ear and rubbed a thumb across my cheek.

"I think you're ready for it. He's always had a great deal of wisdom for me," Mama said. I nodded and flipped the pages quickly.

"Try the 'Master Speed,' or 'Moon Compasses.'" She picked up a moon shell and tucked it into my hand. "I know you'll like that one."

Gram rolled toward us and stopped. Then she pushed sleeping Izzy back and forth.

"Don't forget mine!" she said. Mama reached into the bag and pulled out a second wrapped package. I set Robert Frost and the moon shells down in the sand and took the gift between my hands. I loosened the wrapping paper, letting it fall onto my crossed legs. I tilted the box so I could see the writing. Tin Can Robot, it said. Do It Yourself. I gasped; this was just like the kids in the competition. I grabbed the lid.

"Hold on now, there's another," Gram said, gesturing toward the bag.

Mama pulled out another book. This one was called Building Your Robot from Scratch. I jumped up. "Thanks, Gram," I said, rushing in for a hug. "I love it."

I heard Mama let out an exasperated sigh. "You're good at making her like what you like."

"Hush now," Gram said. "The only thing I'm good at is knowing what both of your interests are. And encouraging them. My poet and my scientist." She gave my shoulder a squeeze. "Imagine, Lucy, you can compete here when you're twelve. You have a knack for this kind of thinking. I can see it. Maybe you can enter a Google science fair if you get really good, or some other . . ."

Gram went on and on, and the dreams piled up in my brain. I dove back into the sand to grab all my presents, but Mama had picked up the Robert Frost for herself. She held it open on her lap and read.

"'And a masked moon had spread down compass rays

To a cone mountain in the midnight haze.'"

"Mama, that sounds so nice," I said, but I couldn't help working my fingers along the top of the robot box while I was saying it. And by the time we were headed back to the room, I was so tired I forgot all about the moon shell. I left it near the half-eaten cupcake and went to bed with big dreams in my head. Mama and I had a harder time connecting after that birthday. Like two magnets back to back.

We slam into a pothole and I jolt out of my memories. Gram's picture jogs loose and Cam catches it right before it hits Izzy on the head. I blink and attempt to line us up, but this road doesn't have clear lines. It's warped and cracked and there is only a very pale yellow in the center. With the rain, it's hard to tell which section is the middle.

"I could use an extra pair of eyes, Mighty Hawk," I say.

I hear Cam set Gram down on the floor.

"It's just hard to tell the middle because of the rain," I say, squinting. I think I'm on the left side of the line, but I'm not certain.

"I've got you covered," he says, leaning up to look out his window. "You're real good on this side. And this side is the one you have to be careful of because we're most likely to career off the planet if we misjudge."

I take a deep breath. "That's very reassuring," I say, glancing to the edge. Off into the darkness.

"Glad to help, Cap'n," he says.

"Clearly," I say. We drive like this for about forty-five

177

minutes, with Cam looking out his side and me looking out the windshield. Me hanging tight on to the wheel. Counting my breaths. Wishing that big white BotBlock tent was coming around the next bend.

We take it real slow. A couple of cars blaze past us and I hope the rain is helping shield the windows. After a while, the storm starts to lighten up, and we turn onto a road with a nice solid yellow line in the middle. We're in the clear, I think. Of course, that's when I notice the fuel gauge is dipping dangerously close to the red line.

"We're getting low on gas," I say.

"We're not too far off, now," Cam says, hitting a minus sign on the GPS screen. He sucks in a breath.

"Uh, we better not risk it. It says we still have twenty minutes to go."

My heart picks up a beat as I think about going into a gas station, where people might recognize us. Might have heard the story. Might call us in and end the game before our moment.

"How much do you think it takes to fill this?" he asks.

"We don't have to fill it, we just need to put in enough to get us twenty minutes down the road. We have to be quick. You got twenty-five from D-Wayne. How much do we have overall and how much can we spend without cutting into our registration money?"

He leans over the arm of the passenger seat, over Izzy and behind my chair. He pulls the paint bucket and a second later, I hear the snap of the rubber band hitting his wrist. He counts under his breath as he peels a few bills off.

"We can spend just over fifteen on gas," he says. I hear the rubber band go back around the money and he tosses it into the paint can.

"He shoots, he scores!" Cam shouts, raising his arms. "And the crowd goes wild. McKinney is one in a million!" He makes a hissing sound that echoes like a crowd of people cheering.

"You can celebrate later. We need to figure out where the heck a gas station is," I say.

We're cruising down some windy strip of road. Dark houses sprinkle the landscape on our right and left. No restaurants or convenience stores to speak of, much less a gas station. We pass a shack that says Barney's Burger Palace. Only it is a tiny place, barely the size of a shed, and the windows are all boarded up. Seems like it would be a good place for a gas station.

Cam hits the GPS. "I think some of these things have places of interest. Richie Frank liked to stop for McDonald's all the time, so we did a lot of searching for those in every town."

"Do what you can, Mighty Hawk."

He punches a button and the color in the cockpit goes from light blue to dark blue.

"All right," he mutters. "Points of interest. Is that the same thing?"

"Sounds like tourist attractions to me," I say.

"Nope. I got it. Fuel."

I hear a *blip blip* as he searches. "Target acquired, Cap'n." *Blip blip.* "Nearest gas station is five miles away."

"Turn right in 0.2 miles," the British lady says as we reroute. I push the brakes slightly and get us going nice and slow nearing the turn. We go right and then left, and right again. Winding our way through a small neighborhood. I hear a dog bark in the distance and hold my breath. We're aliens in enemy territory. All the houses are dark, and feel like they get closer to us the farther we drive. I take a left onto Route 3 and I see the glimmer of a Gulf sign glowing out of the dark. A little dot in the distance.

"Here goes nothing," I say.

"We there yet?" My heart nearly hits the top of my skull. It's Izzy. She pulls her thumb out of her mouth with a pop.

"You get any rest?" Cam asks.

"Turning is making my stomach sore," she says. As I push the brake, I think that despite trying to put on a brave face, going toward this gas station is making my stomach a little bit sore, too. The neon sign gets bigger every second. I find myself pushing the brake, slowing us down twenty miles per hour below the speed limit. I cannot be afraid.

"Mighty Hawk, can you do the fill-up, so I can be prepared in case we need a quick takeoff?" I say.

"Affirmative, Cap'n. I wouldn't have it any other way."

"All right then. Here goes." I squeeze the brake all the way to the floor, put on the blinker, and turn into the Gulf station.

Twenty-Eight

As we roll into the station, I try to line the RV up with the gas pump, starting and stopping a couple times until I think it might be close enough to reach. I push it into park and turn off the engine. My courage drains down my throat and disappears somewhere below my shoes when I look across the parking lot into the store and spot the TV up above the cash register. I can see Cam eyeing it, and despite him holding his chin up high, he is licking his lips an awful lot. He's scared, too. I scan the parking lot. One other car is parked next to the Dumpster. But it's virtually abandoned otherwise.

"Hold on," I say as Cam unclips his buckle. "Queen Nomony, can you go and get the walkie-talkies out of my duffel bag?"

Izzy sits up, picks up the braided wire crown that must have fallen off while she was asleep, and readjusts it on her head. Then she disappears behind the curtain.

"If anything seems strange, anything at all, you let me know."

I hear Izzy unzip the duffel.

"All right, but let's keep it under the radar. We need a code. . . ." Cam snaps, trying to think.

"Maybe 'Mayday'?" I say, thinking that is what they use when ships are going down.

Cam scowls at me. "That doesn't sound suspicious at all."

Izzy comes back through the curtain and hands a walkie to me and a walkie to Cam. I turn the knob so that mine is on. Cam does the same.

"How about 'all is grand,'" he says. "That way, if someone overhears, they won't think anything of it."

"Perfect. We'll keep watch. If something happens, I'll say 'all is grand' and you run around and jump in. Okay?"

He clips the walkie to the top of his shorts, takes a deep breath, and opens the door. "Out into the dangerous night the bravest man ever known . . ." I hear him say as he descends the steps. I set my walkie down between my knees, and Izzy climbs into the passenger seat. Cam closes the door and we watch as he makes his way around the front of the RV.

"You keep an eye on the road," I say, pointing out to where we came in. "Just in case there's a cop looking for us." She leans her head against the door and looks out.

I turn back toward the convenience store. A little neon puddle in an otherwise dark frontier.

"Lucy," Izzy says.

I glance over at her. Her ponytail has dissolved into a big knotted nest held in only by the wire crown.

"What's up?" I ask.

"When will we have the country house Mama was talking about?"

I reach over to squeeze her shoulder. "Soon," I say. I don't want to tell her not for a long, long time. I don't want to tell her to be realistic. "You know how you have to work hard in Mrs. Sunberry's class?"

She nods.

"And what happens when you do all your hard work?" My fingers start to undo a knot poking out the side.

"She gives me a sticker on my chart," she says.

"And . . . ," I say, hearing a thunk. I look in the rear-view, but everything seems fine. Cam's just putting the nozzle in the side of the cab. The gas pump begins to ding.

"Sometimes I get a prize," Izzy says.

I turn back to her. "And that's exactly what is going to happen for us. We have to work hard in order to get our prize. To get what we want."

I run my hand through her tangled curls, trying to brush out the knots as I go. She scowls at me. The trailer rocks from side to side. I glance in the rearview mirror again and see Cam has removed the nozzle.

"Just like Mrs. Sunberry's class?" Izzy asks.

"A lot like it." I turn back to her, but I'm looking out at Cam. Something feels different.

"Why's Mama so sad?" Izzy says.

I stare out the window as Cam heads for the shop door. My mouth goes dry.

"Lucy, why is Mama so sad?" I feel Izzy tug on my arm.

I try to get my head around her question as Cam gets to the door, walks in. He has a quick conversation with the guy at the counter and hands him the money.

"Lucy?"

"She's sick in her head," I say. "Now's not the time—hold on."

"What?" Izzy says.

Cam starts walking back out toward the RV. The walkie crackles to life.

"Flying home, Cap'n. All clear."

"Thanks," I say, taking a sigh of relief. I push the walkie onto the side of my pants. A second later Cam opens the passenger-side door and jumps in. Izzy moves to the corner of the seat, giving Cam room.

"Anything weird?" I ask.

"Negative, Cap'n. We're still under the radar."

The RV jostles and I hear a thud.

"What was that?" I say, standing up. A second later, I see Mama walking across the parking lot. Her hair is a mess, one of her shoes is tied and the other isn't. She's wearing her big jacket and she gets brighter and brighter as she gets to the store. Cam's jaw is nearly on the ground.

"What's she doing?" I hiss.

She goes through the door and straight to the back of the store, picking up a basket.

"Does she think she's going shoppi—"

"Oh no," Cam says, climbing into the middle. I know where he's going to look before he even gets there and my blood turns to ice. He reaches down and then pulls the paint bucket into my view. I look into the interior. Empty. The money for Mission Control.

"Oh god," I say, the air going out of me. I stand, but grab the seat as my whole world spins. I kick off the foot extension.

"She's going to blow all our money," I gasp. All of a sudden it's like I have flashes of light going off inside my head.

I gotta go after her. I reach over my seat and grab the door handle. But just as I am about to slip out of the car, someone knocks on the RV door. I slowly slide into the front seat. My heart hammers in my throat. The knock comes again. Cam points toward the door in the back of the RV. I look across the parking lot. Mama's inside. And someone is at the door.

Twenty-Nine

"YOU STAY RIGHT HERE, OKAY?" I say, making sure Izzy is sitting in the passenger seat. I close the curtain. "Don't make a squeak. Cam, you stay with her." Cam shakes his head.

"No, I gotta stop her." He runs his hand over the top of his head. "I gotta go and get her."

There's another knock. Cam grabs the handle of the passenger door. "Listen," I say, "just . . . keep your head down and don't make a scene, okay?" He nods and jumps out.

I take a deep breath, go into the back, and step down the steps. I grasp the handle. Here goes nothing. I fling the door open and stop. It's not a cop. It's not a whole brigade of cops. It's just a lady holding on to a baby. The baby fusses against her chest.

"I'm so, so sorry to bother you," the mother says, looking up at us from the bottom of the stairs. "I, this is so stupid, but, it's just, we're going back to Derry and we got delayed. I had a bottle for the baby, but he won't take it cold. I'd hate to waste it. I was wondering if I could warm it up. It won't take more than a minute."

Don't act suspicious, Lucille, I think, wishing my world would stop spinning.

"Oh, of course you can," I say, stepping quickly out of the way. "Of course."

She walks up the stairs. I go to the back and pull open the door where I found the other pan. Then stop.

"Oh, the water pump is broken," I say. "Don't you need water for that?"

The woman lets her purse swing under her arm. "That's all right. I have a water bottle. If you don't mind." She pulls out a Poland Spring bottle and hands it to me. I unscrew the cap, pour the water into a pan, and put it onto the stovetop. I flip the burner to medium.

"Thank you so much," the woman says. All of a sudden there is another knock on the door and before I can say anything the lady just goes and opens it. A man appears in the doorway.

"It's all set, babe," the woman says. "These fine folks said they'd warm up the bottle. Be out in a jiff." The man looks around the inside of the camper and I quickly turn away from him in case he's seen my face on the news.

"Much obliged to you," I hear him say from behind me.

"Oh, don't worry," I say, waving to the side.

"Well, I'll run inside and grab that cuppa I was waiting for," he tells his wife. "I'll meet you at the car, or come check if you guys aren't there when I get back."

"Should only take five minutes," she says. Then she pulls the bottle out of her bag and hands it to me. I set it into the water, wondering if I'm doing it right. She doesn't correct me, so I assume it's okay.

"I'm really so sorry to intrude," the mom says. I give her my best look of nonchalance and take a towel from the mini-fridge and wipe down the counters.

The baby lets out a cry and the lady makes clicking noises at it, shifting him so he's laying his head on her chest. She kisses the side of his head and pats his back. I wonder if my mama did that. And if she did, I think, good luck, kid. You don't know what's in store for you, now.

I sit on the end of the couch and look out toward the convenience store, looking for my mama, but I can't see her, not from this angle. I wonder if Cam is having any luck getting her outside. Getting the Mission Control fund back. My heart is pounding so hard, I chance a look down to make sure there isn't an imprint of it there on my chest.

The water bubbles, steam rising around the bottle. The lady stands up and pulls the bottle from the pan. A few droplets spatter off the bottom and sizzle on the stovetop. She shakes it and tests it on her wrist. I glance out across the parking lot again.

"That feels about right," the lady says.

"Oh, good," I say, getting up and flipping the burner off.

She shifts the baby again and I watch as she pops the bottle into the baby's mouth. He sucks hungrily.

"Thanks so much. You're a life saver," the lady says as she makes her way back to the door.

"Sure," I say, trying to breathe. "Sure. Glad to help."

She walks down the steps and out into the night. And I watch them go. That mom, so worried about something as silly as the temperature of milk. That mom fussing over her baby.

The door opens a second later. And there's my mama, and Cam rushing in behind her.

"I couldn't," Cam says.

Mama pushes past me with a brown paper bag in her arms. A bunch of change, crumpled, falls down onto the floor at her feet. She steps over it, scattering the money as she makes her way toward the back. The trail of dollars skitter out behind her. She sets the bag down and starts pulling out bottles. Alcohol, soda. Bags of chips. Some weird moose souvenir. A gallon of maple syrup. I lean down and I pick up the change. Leaf through it. Let it drop. About fifty dollars. The rest gone. The rest of Mission Control fund . . . gone. Everything we worked hard for, all the hopes and dreams of securing a future gone in a couple of market items. I blink my eyes, wishing it weren't true. I see the crumpled bills and picture Gram's face. I can feel her fingers clutching my hand. I hear her voice telling me to promise and I hear myself replying back. I kick a bill across the room, my insides melting into magma.

"Why?" I say.

She doesn't move.

"Why?!" I shout.

Mama doesn't seem to hear me. She mutters to herself

as she fills up a cup and stumbles toward the back room again.

"Listen to me. For once!" I shout. "Do you even hear me?" I feel Cam's hand on my shoulder and shrug it off.

"Why do you do this to us!? We're trying to fix . . . EVERYTHING. And you—you're so *useless*."

Mama's eyes snap up. Filled with tears. All of a sudden her ears are working?

"You know something," I spit. "With any other god-damned mom, we would just go to the stupid robot competition and go home and go to bed. Easy. But not with you. Not with you." I point at her. "Nothing can be easy with *you*. Run. Steal. See things that don't exist. Do you have a brain at all? Or are you just a stupid empty shell?"

Cam's hand squeezes my shoulder. "We gotta beat it. I think—I think they know who we are." But I can't move. My dreams are littered in front of me. Space junk, bouncing around in the void.

"The whole time, I try to help," I say, "Why don't you do something to help for a change?" I see Mama's eyes light up with tears.

"What?" she hisses.

"You're a joke."

Cam grabs my arm as I hear footsteps echo on the pavement outside.

"They're coming," he says. "Please."

A siren wails in the distance.

I drop sideways into the driver's seat. The convenience

store man runs around the side of the RV. I jam my foot extension on and slam the key forward in the ignition. The engine fires to life. I hear Cam locking the door as we speed off onto the main road. I hear the sirens somewhere behind us. And I drive forward. I hear something tip over and fall in the back. Maybe it's Mama. I don't care. Not anymore. I don't care about anything. 'Cause it's useless. We're all useless. And Mr. Blinks was right. The whole time. Sunnyside is a black hole of a place. And everyone knows that if you get stuck in a black hole, you don't have a chance. You get torn to pieces.

Thirty

We wind our way down small roads that lead farther and farther from the sirens. I take random turns. "Recalculating, recalculating," the British lady says, but I ignore her until I can't hear sirens anymore.

She recalculates one more time and we're back on Route 101, heading to Seahook. The rain stops and a few stars start to speckle the sky in front of us. I wonder if Mama is in the back, drinking enough alcohol to kill herself. I don't pull the car over to check.

"Maybe we could get some more money when we get there?" Cam says.

"Yeah," I say. "Yeah, right. By stealing it? I don't want to steal anything else."

"Stealing's bad," Izzy says, pulling her thumb out of her mouth just long enough to say it.

"No," Cam says. "Maybe we could use PingPing to find some—"

"To find three hundred dollars?" I say through gritted teeth. "You're crazier than she is." My throat catches and I don't mean for my sentence to come out as mean and sharp as it does. But it's there, and it hangs in the air between us.

"Please." Cam's voice is strained. It's the wimpiest voice I've ever heard and I want to smack it out of him. It's the opposite of Mighty Hawk. It's who he is, not who he wants to be. No matter what, we're both stuck with that.

"We have to try," Cam says.

I squeeze the steering wheel, pretty much fed up with his positive thinking. I push back the pressure that seems to be forming behind my eyes.

"I did! I tried. I always try." I feel a tear slip down my cheek and blink it fast so I can see the road in front of us. "Why didn't you, Cam? Why didn't you hide the paint can? Why didn't you get Mama out of the store? It'll work if you try hard enough, right? If you want it hard enough? So why didn't you get her, Cam." I wipe my face.

It's silent in the RV then. Silent besides Cam's sniffling. When I look over, I see a tear sliding down his cheek. And it makes my heart twist. But I don't care. Because we're all a bunch of losers and the sooner he realizes that, the better.

We're silent as we make our way onto Route 1A. The ocean spreads out to our left. A big, dark, rolling mass in the night. I recognize where we are now as we head into Seahook. I slam on the brakes as we get to corners and stop signs. There are a few cars out, going through town, and I figure every single person probably knows who we are. I don't care. I don't care if we get pulled over and the cops drag us all away. And I'll go to foster scare. And Mama'll go to Kensington. And I won't see her for the rest of my life. And that'll be just fine as far as I'm concerned. I hear Izzy start sniffling, there next to Cam, and my heart squeezes in my chest.

"Destination on right in 0.2 miles," the British lady says. My heart doesn't soar. It plummets as we hit the green. I see the big white tent. No tables are set up yet, but the tent is there, and I see the BotBlock Jr. sign in the light of the streetlamps. I slam the RV over to the right, trying to squeeze it into a parking spot that is way too small. I misjudge the distance to the curb so we lurch forward as one of our tires goes up onto the sidewalk.

"Well, we're here," I say, unclipping my buckle. It whips across my waist. Izzy squirms in Cam's lap and sits up. She looks from me to Cam and then out the window.

"Is it Mission Control time?" she asks.

"Nah," I tell her. "That's over."

She looks at Cam. His face crinkles up. "It can't be over," he says. "This was our dream. Thi—" He stops, and I see his jaw twitch as his teeth grind together.

"Well, we tried and we failed," I say. "Mission not accomplished. That's it. Accept it."

I get up to walk through the curtain, a dollar bill crunching under my foot.

"Lucy," Cam says, his voice so small behind me.

"Here." I lean down and pick up the crumpled bills.

"Take it, Cam. Take it and get your membership and get out of here. Run as far away from us as you can. We're so messed up." The tears stream down my face now. "Give yourself a chance and get away from us." I push him to the door.

"Cap—"

"Don't," I say. "You can't do anything to help us. But you can help yourself. Get out of here."

"We're in this together," he whispers.

I let go of the money and it drops down his chest and into his hands.

"Leave no ma—" he starts.

"Stop. This isn't a game. You'll be better off." I push his shoulder toward the door. We lock eyes, but I don't budge. Not one bit, and he backs out onto the sidewalk, the door swinging closed behind him.

"What's happening?" Izzy says, looking out the windshield. "Where's Cam going?"

"Nowhere," I say. "Just like the rest of us."

I see him out the front windshield for a moment, looking at the money in his hand. He looks at me and I shake my head, and he turns and disappears down the sidewalk. I wipe my eyes and face Mama. She's a shadow, a lump of darkness in the back corner of the RV. And there's something at her feet. I try to blink my tears out, wondering if they are what I think they are. I reach up and feel for the dome light. Flip it on.

Pill bottles. She's got one gripped in her hand and the rest are scattered at her feet. Pills form little puddles around her toes.

"Now you're going to take your pills? Jesus Christ," I say, going over to her. I pick up the bottles at her feet. "Now that you're out there, *now* you're going to start taking them?"

"Did you see Rob? Did you see the farm?" she mutters.

"No," I say, "I didn't see a darn thing." I pick the pill bottle up and then push the pills into my hand. Stop.

They don't feel right. I lean so that my head isn't casting a shadow onto my hands. The ceiling light pools over my open palms. Beans. Dried beans.

"What's this?" I say.

Mama doesn't respond to me, but she keeps on talking. "I could write a poem for the end of the world."

I drop the handful and grab another bottle, overturning it. They're not pills. More dried beans.

"What?" I take the one from her hand, unprying her fingers. I peer inside. My head is on fire. I feel like a supergiant, a massive angry star, on the verge of collapsing inward. I try to catch my breath. But I can't. I throw the bottle and dried beans skitter out into the aisle, bounce against one another and ping off the table leg.

"Leave it alone," Mama says, seeming to snap out of it for a second. "I said leave it alone."

"Why are your bottles filled with beans?" I shout. "Why would you do that? Are you trying to ruin everything?"

She twists the bottle out of my hand.

"Mama, Lucy, stop, please," Izzy says from the front.

"I said leave it alone!" Mama shouts, standing up, taller than me now. The heat inside me starts to build. I pull the bottle back and fling it to the side. It bounces and clatters against the tabletop behind me.

"Someone is looking in the window," Izzy whispers. "Please stop fighting." But I don't even turn and look. 'Cause let them come.

Mama's eyes get real big. "We better destroy the evidence." She spots a picture on the wall and reaches for it. Her lips are ringed with red. They look dry standing out against her wet face. It's the ugliest thing I've ever seen.

"Stop!" I say, reaching for the picture. "Explain to me why these bottles are filled with beans." I pick up a bottle and flip it over. The beans skitter down like a waterfall. Mama stops my hand. Grabs my arm. The force squeezes tears out of my eyes and the breath out of my lungs.

"You. Stop it! You listen to me," she says. A little pool of spit forms in the corner of her lips, and my whole body runs cold. Slows down.

"Don't tell me what to do," my voice growls, lower than I've ever heard it before. "You of all people can't tell me what to do. You're a lost cause."

I see her eyes go bright and she releases me, but I'm already pulling, so I fly toward the front and down the stairs, my arm colliding with the wood at the end of the couch. Izzy rushes toward me and gets caught in the tangle of my legs, landing hard on my stomach. My back hits the edge of the stairs. The wind goes out of me.

As I look up, I feel like I'm not a part of me. Like I'm seeing this all as a spectator. Mama yanks the picture off the wall. It spins from her hand, onto the floor, skidding among the beans. Bouncing from one corner of the frame to the other. Landing with a crack against the table leg. The glass fractures with a pop. Mama folds into a ball, her hands rising up around her ears as her body lowers to the floor. I blink back tears. Begin to find my way back into my body. Izzy's hand is holding on so tightly to my shirt that she's also got hold of my skin. Like a metal pincher, it begins to unclamp as I rise up. My face goes from numb to throbbing. My ears ring and then clear to the sound of sirens. A gush seems to soar through my body as my lungs take in air. Izzy bounces and pulls herself up, crying. I scramble to my feet.

"Let's go." I push myself up and slam the door open. Someone on the street runs. I don't see who it is. I just hear the footsteps retreating. That's a good idea, I think. I turn back, and PingPing looks at me with his LED eyes. I reach in, grab hold of him.

"Climb on," I hear myself saying. Izzy jumps from the stairs onto my back and we go. I don't know where we're going. I don't care. I'd rather be on my own than taking care of mad Mama for one more minute. The sirens get louder and we slip away.

Thirty-One

I RUN AND RUN AND RUN. The blue and white flashing lights rush like a flood behind us. The only path I follow is one marked by shadows. I dodge up a sidewalk, Izzy feeling so much bigger than she used to be. At the corner of Ocean and Birch, we duck down a side street and Izzy slides off my back. We run away from the ocean, toward a wooded park. I pull the gate open. A plaque says SEAHOOK GARDEN CLUB. Just inside is a little shed. I grab the lock. It comes loose in my hand and I pull it off. Izzy ducks in and I set PingPing down. I inhale deeply, wipe my forehead, try to clear my eyes. Try to clear my mind. I take three fast breaths. It smells like flowers and soil in here. I pull over a bag of mulch and try to fluff it like a pillow. I set Izzy down so she is lying with her head on it. And I hear the sirens off in the distance. I picture them taking Mama. I picture Cam turning away. I picture me shouting. I grab the hair on both sides of my head, sink down, and try to reason this out.

"Lucy?" Izzy says, leaning into me. I feel her small fingers trying to wrap around mine. But I'm holding on to my hair too tight. "Lucy, are we going to be okay?" she asks. I tell myself to suck it up. I take a big swallow and grasp her fingers.

"Time for bed," I say, wiping my face. I lie down with my head on the mulch bag and Izzy tucks in to me. She shakes in my arms and I squeeze her tight. Trying to get her to calm down, too. We're better off on our own. We're better off now than we ever were. That's what I tell myself.

"Are you afraid, Queen Nomony?" I whisper, rubbing her arm.

"I wanna go ho-ome," she says with a hiccup.

I wrap my arm around her and press my cheek to her cheek. "I know. Do you want to hear about the time Juniper Ray and Mighty Hawk faced down the evil Bachmans?"

Izzy shakes her head. "No."

"How about the time Juniper Ray and Mighty Hawk caught the Swampvonk? Or maybe the time Queen Nomony saved the Tinktree people?"

"No," Izzy says. "I just wanna go home."

I tuck her hair back so it's not making a wet mat between our cheeks. "Well, first things first," I say, trying to make my voice steady and strong. "You need rest for the journey. Three deep breaths."

We take one breath in together. Then another.

"Last one," I say, and I feel her belly expand and then deflate. "That a girl."

We do that five more times. In and out. Each one a little longer than the last. And after an eternity, the shuddering stops and Izzy falls asleep. But not me. As much as I close my eyes, I got a battery full of juice and I don't think I'll ever power down. I think about the mission. I replay the argument with Mama over and over again. I send Gram a faraway hug and tell her I wish she were here to help sort this out. To help take care of everything. I tell her a million times I'm sorry we let her down and that it was Mama getting in the way of everything as usual. Then I hit the ground with my fist, fed up with everyone, including myself. I count to one hundred in my head, trying to force myself to sleep. I count to two hundred, picturing the numbers on the backs of my eyelids. I pretend I can hear Mr. Blinks's banjo strings plucking out a lullaby. But nothing works. The peepers outside are too loud. The ocean roars in the distance. Cars drive by and the headlights wash the walls with sparks of light. I can't get my head to stop talking. Are they coming for us? What are we going to do now? What will they do to Mama? What will Cam do? I sit up and stare at the wheel of a lawnmower, and I wonder where he is. I shouldn't have sent him away. Why did I have to get so hotheaded?

If we're all on the run, we might as well be on the run together, but I screwed that up, too.

Izzy rolls over, hitting me with her leg. Something jabs my hip. I think she's got her crown in her pocket, but then I see it's on her head. She shifts again and I get another jab to the side. I reach down, and my hand lands on the top of the walkie-talkie. I yank it off my pants, and as I do, I accidentally press the button. The sound of static crackles through the shed. I dial the volume down low. I check Izzy. She moves her head a little, but stays asleep.

I turn the knob on the top of the walkie-talkie the teensiest bit and put my mouth up to it. I squeeze the talk button ever so lightly, hoping to heck that Cam still has his.

"Mighty Hawk, this is Juniper Ray," I say quietly. "Do you copy?"

I let go of the button, move so I am sitting on top of the bag of soil. I lean up against the wall of the shed and hold the walkie next to my ear. Nothing but fuzz.

"Mighty Hawk," I say, wiping my nose. My voice drops to normal. "Yeah, uh, Cam, this is Lucy. I'm sorry. I-I hope you're—where are you?"

My hand releases the button and I take a deep breath in. A breath that seems to shake the whole shed. I wait for a response. Wait and hope. Wait some more. When no response comes, I squeeze the button one last time.

"I'm—I'm sorry. Over and out."

The silence wraps around me. In the dark of the shed, with not a friend in the universe, the tears chase each other down my face like rovers over the surface of the moon. I rock my head against the wall, feeling the grain of the wood roll against the back of my skull. No, no, no. Over and over again. No, no, no. I close my eyes and try to will the walkie to life. But the silence coming out of it is the kind you'd expect at the edge of the universe. I look at PingPing, a round lump in the corner.

"We gave it our best," I say. I set the walkie down next

to me and stare up at the ceiling. "We just weren't good enough—" The walkie crackles to life, just as I am thinking this is typical. I grab it and pull it to my ear.

"Lucy, where are you? It's Cam."

I press the button, jumping up to my knees. "Cam, you okay?" I whisper.

"I'm okay," he says. "Are you guys okay?"

"Yeah, we're three blocks from downtown. In some garden club shed. Where are you?"

"Somewhere on the beach."

I get up and step over to the door. "Can you head out of town?" I close my eyes, imagining the best way to describe where we are. In all our visits to Seahook, we've only come to the garden club once. "You know where we stopped?"

"Yeah," he says.

"Go up toward the Dunkin' Donuts and then take a right on Main and head out of town."

"The cops are sweeping at the center." *Ppshhhhh.* "But I think I can skirt around. I'll see you soon." *Ppshhhhh.*

"You should see the gate. Then come to the back of the flower garden," I say, hoping I'm still coming through clear. "It's labeled."

"I'll be" *pssshhhh* "-ere," he says.

I get up and start pacing, checking the park every time I pass the door. I count to sixty, ten times, and then see a shadow flit by the pond. I inch the door open. Something dodges behind a tree, then rolls, then a second later, Cam is standing there in front of me. He rushes in.

"I'm sorry," I say real quiet, wrapping him in a hug. He squeezes me tight.

"I'm sorry, too," he says. "I'm sorry I lost the money."

"It wasn't your fault. It's hard to stop Mama when she makes up her mind about something."

"Maybe," he says, pulling back. "Either way, it's gone."

"And we're here," I say.

He looks down and spots Izzy on the ground and I see him scan the rest of the shed. Over the gardening equipment and the lawn mower. We sit down against a few bags of mulch. I scoop Izzy up and pull her in toward me.

"Camrin here?" she asks, waking halfway.

"Right here," he says, wrapping his arm around her shoulder. I wrap my arm around the other side of Izzy, so we're holding her in the middle. And we close our eyes and, finally, fall into a fitful sleep.

Thirty-Two

Beep-beep beep-beep. I START AWAKE. LIFTING my face off my arm. The first thing I notice is that I can feel my heart. I can feel it weighing heavy in every part of my body, like I went to sleep a human and woke up an open nerve. It hurts to blink, but I force my eyes open and closed, cracking the dust from my eyelashes.

Beep-beep beep-beep. I reach toward the sound. My watch. It's nine o'clock. T-minus—I squeeze the buttons hard and shut it up. It pinches my skin as I press down, and I take the strap, pull it loose, and toss it into the corner. Who needs it when I got nowhere to go, anyway?

I look up to see Izzy staring at me. With the sun streaking in through the sideboards, her ratty hair is making a halo around her head. There are purple marks under her eyes, like she's been in a fight with the sandman. Her face is smudged with dirt trails, too. I wipe at her cheek, but it smudges the dirt across it, leaving a dark smear toward the bridge of her nose.

"How you doing, Queen Nomony?" I say.

She tries for a smile, but looks away. Cam gets up and

stretches. Then slumps back into the mulch as he looks around the shed, remembering where we are.

"Mighty Hawk, I've assessed the situation," I say. Cam raises his eyebrows. "It is dire."

The silence that follows is enough to tell me that they both agree. I hear the waves and the sound of BotBlock starting. Loudspeakers, the humming of happy people, the savory grease-soaked smells of the food tent off in the distance. My stomach growls. I turn my head and put my eyes up to the slit between the boards. It's quiet here. A few bumblebees flit around a bed of yellow flowers and out over a koi pond. I stare at all the colors.

"I have to go potty," Izzy says.

"Okay," I say, making myself get up.

"You think it's safe going out there?" Cam says.

I step toward him, offering my hand. He grabs it and hops up.

"Probably not," I say as we release. "But we can't stay in here all day. If we're caught in here, it's obvious who we are. If we're blending in with a bunch of other kids"—I look out toward the direction of the din—"maybe not so obvious?"

"And since we have a robot." Cam goes to PingPing, unwraps the remote control from his neck, and hands it to me.

"Right," I say, taking the controller. "We have a good chance of blending in, for a little while."

Cam turns PingPing on and I flip the little switch on the RC. Lights blink. *Wuw-whir, wuw-whir.*

"Morning, buddy," I say, steering him to me.

Cam goes over to the door and opens it a crack. Izzy finds her way to him. "We got picnic tables and koi ponds to the starboard side," Cam says.

I string the remote control lanyard around my neck, then look out between the slats on my side. "Just flowers over here."

We pile up at the door and I see Izzy is starting to get the wiggles. She really has to go. "Can you hold it five minutes? Long enough for us to get down to BotBlock?"

"I think so," Izzy says. Her knees start to jump.

"That a girl," I say, putting my hand on her back.

Cam slides the door open. The sunlight beams in, leaving a golden trail across the shed. He sticks his head out and looks both ways. Then he nods and we duck out behind him. I steer PingPing so he's bopping along next to us. And I can't help but notice, he's running pretty good. Faring better than the rest of us on this adventure. That's for sure. We go to the gate and slip through. I steer Ping-Ping down the sidewalk.

"Act casual," I say.

Izzy skip-steps so she doesn't land on a crack in the sidewalk. Cam pushes his hands into his pockets, and I lead us the busiest way back into town, hoping to get wrapped up in a crowd. We take a right onto Main Street and walk, past cafés, clothing stores, tourists, and candy shops. And when we turn onto Ocean Avenue, the green and the beach come into view. The RV is gone. Nothing looks unsettled. Kids line up at the registration tables and everything goes on as it should.

"This way," I say, ducking into the middle of the green, between a swarm of kids doing a test run. I scan the field and spot the Porta-Potties. Izzy spots them, too, and breaks into a run. Cam, PingPing, and I hurry after her. They're all lined up in a row. Most say *vacant* in green on the knob. I let the RC swing around my neck and open the first one for her. She dives in.

"I'll wait for you right here," I say. "Let me know if you need anything."

She closes the door behind her and Cam goes into the one next to it. I lean against the corner and keep a lookout.

"Blake, stand in front of that tree there," a lady with curly red hair says. A boy with the same curly red hair rolls his eyes but he steps toward the tree, just like she asks. His dad brings his robot over to him and sets it down by his side. I've never seen so many smiles. The mom and dad have these huge grins on their fat faces. Their teeth shine in the sun. The boy looks a little annoyed, but I know deep down, he's going to remember this day for the rest of his life. And I half laugh because it's funny, sitting here watching this, that at one time, I thought I could have any part of it. I check the field, seeing if I can spot the junkbot competition, but there are too many kids, seas of heads and shoulders blocking my view of the arenas.

A breeze blows, carrying the smell of sausage, peppers, and onions across the green. My stomach growls again, reminding me that the chili was too long ago. I scan to the left and spot the food tent. I can see the back of three big metal carts. We have fifty dollars. That's good for more than one meal. More than enough for lunch. Dinner, too. Then, who knows what.

The door opens and Izzy steps out.

"You wash your hands?" I say.

"Tantarizer," she says, rubbing her hands together.

"Yes, sanitizer," I say, wondering why she can never get that word.

Cam steps out a moment later. "I'll hang with Izzy," he says. I unloop the remote control from my neck. Hand it over and go in the first Porta-Potty. Before I close the door, I notice a kid walk by and point at Izzy. I swallow hard. Her hair has been collecting knots and dust since we started.

"Cam," I hiss, hanging off the door.

He turns. "Can you, maybe pull her hair into a ponytail or something?"

"Got it, Cap'n," Cam says. He gives me an A-OK sign.

I go in and close the door. As I'm trying not to let the backs of my legs touch the Porta-Potty seat, I spot myself in the dingy mirror. I see my hair is a complete mess, too. Between the rain and the dust, I seem to have a cloud around me. I rub a smudge on my collar, and somehow it seems to get darker the longer I try to get it off. I finish up and squirt some of the hand sanitizer into my palm, rub it around, and then wipe my hands off with a paper towel.

Then I put a little hand sanitizer on the towel and smear it across my face. It feels all wet and gushy as it hits my cheek, but I rub until the dirt is gone. I wipe around my eyes and along the bridge of my nose. I can't help but make a face as the slimy liquid squishes toward my hairline. Bleh. I rub the rest into my hands and then pull back the pieces of hair around my face. I pull the band out of my hair and work the pieces back up into a ponytail.

"Is that your robot?" I hear muffled voices through the door and twist the tie back around my hair as quickly as I can.

"Yep," Cam says.

"Look at that piece of junk," another kid says. The hair tie snaps against my finger and I stop and strain to listen as their voices get quiet.

"Delusional," I hear them say as they pass close to the vent. The word rings in my ears. I open the door fast.

Cam's nostrils are flaring. He's holding Izzy's hair up in a point and he's glaring them down as they walk away.

My face is on fire and I feel like my heart is splaying open on its hinges.

"Idiots," Cam says, going back to twisting the rubber band around the base of Izzy's ponytail.

"Yeah," I say, stepping out of the bathroom. "Idiots."

"Idiots," Izzy yells. Cam twirls the rubber band for the last time and looks up at the sky, shaking his head. I can't help but laugh. I try to cover it up so Izzy knows I don't approve, but it feels good to giggle for a minute.

"What do you think?" Cam asks, pointing Izzy toward me. Her hair is a big mess, but at least now it is looking a little bit more curly and a little bit less like there is a family of rats living in it.

"Perfect. You hungry?" I nod toward the food tent.

"I am." Izzy's hand shoots into the air.

"Starved," Cam says.

We follow our noses around the perimeter and find some grub.

Thirty-Three

WE SIT ON A WALL A few yards from the food tent and dig in. The sausage seems to explode into my mouth, the spices and grease warming my throat. Izzy takes a big bite, which is only about half the size of mine. I watch her cheeks work like a chipmunk. I swallow and then lick my napkin and try to get the smudge off her cheek. She gives me a scowl and pushes my hand away.

"There, it's a little better now," I say, getting one more swipe in.

She continues to munch.

"Good?" I sit down on the stone wall.

"Mmmhhmmmm," she says, scooting close to me.

Cam swallows the last bite of his before I get halfway through mine.

"Think I can get another one?" he says.

I nod. "Of course," I say, crunching through a red pepper. "Get me another one, too."

"All right," Cam says, standing up. "Izzy, you want another?"

She shakes her head, looking at all the sausage on her

plate. I cut it into chunks, so she could eat one bite-sized piece at a time.

Cam jogs over to the line. A pigeon tries to land on PingPing's head and I can tell he's annoyed by that. I wave it away and it hops from his head onto the wall. Izzy pulls a piece of sausage free and tosses it to him. He pecks at it greedily.

"Where we going?" Izzy says, swallowing a hunk of sausage. She peels another piece out of the roll and shoves it into her mouth.

"Not sure," I say, wiping some grease off on my pants.

She swallows. "Camrin, you, me, and Mama are heading for the country house?"

The sausage roll in my mouth seems to work into a solid mass and head toward my throat. "No, we can't do that now."

She looks at me, her eyebrows knitting into a knot. I put my plate down next to her on the wall. Not hungry all of a sudden.

"You have to win," Izzy says through a mouthful of food. "You have to win, then apologize to Mama, then Mission Control pl—"

"Right," I say, thinking she has really got it backward. I don't know how to explain this to her. I don't know how to tell her that the plan's over. Everything is over. Mama couldn't care less where we are and the sooner she realizes that the better.

Izzy puts the rest of her sausage on her plate, too, and won't pick it up for another bite.

"I wanna go home," she says.

I laugh, but it comes out more like a hiss. More like water hitting a frying pan.

"You wanna go *home*?" I say, leaning down to her.

"Mama," she says.

I feel the heat building up inside me again. "Mama doesn't care if you're alive or dead. I'm the one who takes care of you, anyway."

I see Izzy's eyes brighten up with tears. I feel mine prickling, too.

"We don't have a home. We don't have a mama," I say. "So stop. Okay?"

I see a big fat tear slide down Izzy's cheek.

"Everything all right over here?" A man with a Bot-Block hat appears next to us. I stand up, tuck my hands into my pockets. I don't see a badge or a police uniform, just a colorful hat. Nosy.

"Fine," I say.

He cocks his head to one side and looks from my face to Izzy's. Then I see him look around. When he spots Cam talking to the sausage vendor, he stops. Then turns back to me. I grab Izzy's hand in case I have to run.

"Uh, very well then," he says, holding his hands up and backing away. "Just checking." He hurries off in the other direction. Cam comes up next to us.

"Let's move." I pick up the remote control. Cam grabs

the leftover sausage roll on the wall, tucking it next to the two new ones in his hands.

"What's happening?"

"I don't know," I say, spinning and searching the crowd for the stranger. "This nosy guy. He looked like maybe he recognized us."

Izzy gets up next to me. "I wanna go home."

"Let's go this way, then," I say, knowing I won't be able to trick her for very long. I scan the green, looking for the busiest spot.

"Next in this corner will be junkbots, with tri-bots on deck!" an announcer says. The crowd shifts slightly as some make their way to the junk arena. Cam and I work our way into the center of that crowd and I scan for trouble. The problem is, as I look, I'm seeing about five people with BotBlock hats in the immediate vicinity. Some men, some women. Some looking around, some helping the individual competitions. They're everywhere

I think I spot the nosy guy's sandy hair. "This way," I say, navigating PingPing toward the junkbot arena.

Cam keeps a hand on Izzy's shoulder and I toggle right and left, keeping PingPing out of the way of people's feet. We stop next to the entrance, where kids are busy making adjustments to their junkbots.

"Is that your robot?"

I look to my right. A lady with a BotBlock hat and a clipboard is standing there next to me, pointing at Ping-Ping with the back of her pencil.

"Yeah," I say, following her gaze.

"You must be Lucille." My throat tightens into a knot and Cam's head snaps up.

"What?" I say, wondering if I heard her right.

"You must be Lucille Peevey. You're the last to arrive." I stare at her, a cold flush going through my whole system. My gaze wanders to the sign above her head. REGISTRATION. I wonder if I heard her right. I wonder if I'm dreaming. Is this a trap? When I look at Cam, I can see he is as confused as I am. I step over to the registration table and my eyes fall to the white cloth. There are three unclaimed name tags on the tabletop. TRISTAN GALANDRA, BOT: CLAMCRUSHER under the tri-bots sign. TIM JONES, BOT: THETANK under the mindstorm sign. And then, right there, I put my hand on it. LUCILLE PEEVEY, BOT: PING-PING200 in the junkbot category.

"That's impossible," I say. "I didn't register—early."

The lady looks down at her clipboard. "Lucille Peevey, junior competitor in the junk competition. Bot: Ping-Ping200? I recognized your bot." She points toward Ping-Ping's name, stamped proudly across his chest. She flips a few pages on her clipboard. "Lucille."

"Yeah, uh." I back up and trip over Izzy's foot.

"Ouch," Izzy says, pushing me off.

"Sorry," I say.

"You registered six weeks ago. You should have received confirmation by mail," the lady says. The world seems to tip and turn, like the planet has been knocked off its axis.

"Who registered me? Did Mrs. Shareze register me?" I ask, thinking of that perfect yellow card she gave me on my birthday.

She scans her paper. "Oh, it doesn't say that."

I feel Cam tugging on my arm. "I think— I think we're in trouble," he whispers. The lady in the BotBlock visor looks at him, confused.

"We gotta go." He points toward the sausage vendor. I follow his gaze and see a man with SECURITY written across his chest, staring at us and talking into a walkie-talkie.

"Right," I say. "We gotta go." I spring to the right. I try to bring PingPing with us, but it's obvious to me that we're going to lose him in the crowd. He crashes into a table as we are leaving the junkbot area. And I hate to leave him, but I don't have any other choice. I make a silent promise to come back for him after dark as I let the remote swing around my neck and grab Izzy by the hand. We dodge to the right, to the left. I look over my shoulder. The security guard is coming for us, pushing through the crowd. Cam keeps pace just ahead, clearing the path. All of a sudden a baby carriage is right in front of me. I slam on the brakes and swing to the side so as not to hit it. Izzy and I regain balance just in front of it. At the same time, my shoulder hits a girl. A cup of soda flies out of her hand and explodes on the sidewalk.

"Hurry!" Cam says, stopping and waving us on. The sausages hop in his arms and fall to the ground. I pull Izzy through the spilled drink. Two cops appear on the right. We go left. Two cops there, too. I pull Izzy through the crowd. But everywhere I look, someone is coming toward us. One way, and then the other, until everyone stops what they're doing and stares. My heart clangs against my chest as a lady in a suit appears out of the crowd and holds a badge toward me.

"You're safe now," she says.

But I'm feeling just about as far from safe as we can be. Here in the middle of a crowd, the only barricade between being free and being caught is the garbage skittering across the pavement.

"My name's Ms. Linda and I'm with the New Hampshire Department of Social Services. We're here to help you," the lady says.

Izzy hugs on to my waist and Cam and I stand shoulder to shoulder as the cops form a circle around us.

"If you'll come with us, we can get you some food, water, get you to a safe place . . ." She looks to the side, like she isn't sure if we're going to run and wants to make sure there are enough people to block us if we do. And there are. There are more than enough.

"You've been through a trauma," Ms. Linda says. "When you're ready, we want to get you safe. Get you back home."

I feel Izzy's tight squeeze release from my waist. And

she steps toward Ms. Linda. I reach for her shoulder, but she walks out of my reach. "Izzy, get back here." I squat down, as if she can't hear me from where I am standing.

"Izzy!" Cam shouts, squatting down, too.

"C'mere, Izzy, what are you doing?" I hiss.

"Going home?" Izzy asks as she stops an arm's length from Ms. Linda. I think the cops are gonna run in and grab her, but instead Ms. Linda kneels down and reaches out. Izzy takes the bait. Not loyal. Not at all. Cam and I stand.

"The game's up," Cam says. We link arms. If nothing else, I am staying beside Cam, no matter what. As we walk toward Ms. Linda, a resounding applause breaks out. I'm not even sure what everyone is clapping about. We get ushered into a car. First Cam. I climb in behind him, and sit in the middle. Izzy squirms into the seat next to me. The door closes and we're engulfed in the smell of new plastic and peppermint.

Izzy adjusts and the seat squeaks. "I want Mama," she says.

Ms. Linda eyes us in the rearview mirror.

"First we're going to go to the doctor. Make sure all is well." She looks at me instead of Izzy, but I break her gaze and stare out the window. I see the lady at the registration table. Her eyes are etched with worry. Like she might think this is her fault, somehow. I watch as she leans down and picks up PingPing, then pushes her way through the crowd. A police officer meets her there and I see their heads nod and lips move, but I don't know what they're saying. The officer picks up PingPing and I wonder if they are going to send him somewhere he doesn't want to go either. I reach over Izzy and grab the door handle, but then I see the officer load him into the trunk. At least we're together. Once he's in, I look out and notice most everyone has continued to go about their competitions. The interruption is now over.

The car jolts and slides into motion. I stare down at my hand and realize I'm holding something between my fingers. The sticker. The registration sticker. I flick the edge with my thumb. Someone registered me for the BotBlock. Someone registered me for that stupid challenge. Someone was looking out for me. Someone who actually cares. Maybe Mrs. Shareze. Maybe Mr. Blinks. Someone.

Thirty-Four

AT THE ER THEY CHECK US for scrapes and bruises. The doctor is pretty nice and does reflex tests and promises us lollipops if we're good. It's not like we're going anywhere, I think. No need to bribe.

"They're all in good shape despite a couple of bruises," the doctor says to Ms. Linda. "You'll get my full report within the hour." He hits the clipboard with the back of his fingertips and heads out the door.

Izzy leans close to me and a nurse with curly brown hair pops her head in. "I have a family consultation room all set for you."

Ms. Linda nods. "Thank you." She turns to us. "All right, guys."

"What's a family consultation room?" I ask.

Ms. Linda squats down so she is at our level. "It's where we're going to go and figure out what happens next," she says. "Where we can talk alone and get your full story and make plans that will keep you safe."

"Where's Mama?" Izzy says before I can jump in.

"We're going to talk about that, too." Ms. Linda raises

her hand and squeezes Izzy's arm very gently. "Sound good?"

It only sounds so-so to me, and when I look over at Cam I can see he isn't that thrilled about it either. Even though Ms. Linda is talking real nice, she looks sharp around the edges like she means business. Her suit doesn't have a wrinkle in it, and her hair is straight and pinned up so not even a little wisp could escape if it wanted to.

She stands up and leads us into the hallway. We go past the hospital bedrooms and past some guy moaning in a chair. Two turns later and we're in a section that's more offices than beds. Ms. Linda knocks gently on one of the doors and when there's no reply, she opens it and we go in. It's comfy looking. Two couches, a desk, and a couple of chairs. In between the couches there's a coffee table and someone has set out muffins and juice boxes.

"Take a seat," Ms. Linda says. She picks up an orange juice container, shakes it, and pries it open, then hands it to Izzy.

"Juice?" she says to me.

I pick one up before her hand can get to it. "I can take care of myself, thanks."

Ms. Linda seems to take the hint and leans against the desk. We plop down on the couches. Me and Izzy on one side and Cam on the other. Cam picks up a muffin and starts eating.

"So," Ms. Linda says, pulling out a folder. "I don't

want to rush you guys, but when you're feeling up to it, I'd like to ask you some questions."

"We're feeling fine," I say, taking a sip of the juice. Izzy squirms away from me just the teensiest bit.

Ms. Linda jots something down on the piece of paper. Great, another person writing the story of my life in a manila folder. I look at Cam. I can tell he's reading my mind, because he looks at that pen moving, too, and rolls his eyes. Once Ms. Linda is done scribbling, she sets into the questions. Exact names and dates of birth and how did we get here? What happened from the beginning to the end of it. I go over the whole story, and Cam and Izzy interject the whole time. We tell her everything, from planning to go to BotBlock and getting all ready, to the emergency workers coming to the house, to our big escape, to when Mama got real bad and how we drove halfway, and then to how Mama ruined everything. Some parts Ms. Linda hardly seems to believe. Her eyebrows go up and down like they're on a roller coaster, but the whole time, she keeps writing. Then she asks to talk to Cam alone. Cam braces himself, his feet flat on the floor and his elbows on his bent knees. Keep your head down, I think as Izzy and I get sent out into the hallway.

The same cop who spotted us at BotBlock is there. He's holding PingPing.

"Brought back your friend," he says, dimples forming at both sides of his mouth. Why so cheery, I want to ask him, but instead I just say thanks, real quiet, and flop into the chair. I pull PingPing over to me and put my hand on his head. It's good to have him back again. I pull the remote control from around my neck and place it in its spot around his.

Another cop comes up and goes right into the room with Cam and Ms. Linda. I lean over the chair to see if I can get close enough to hear what's going on. I hear a lot of words, but they're too muffled to string into any sort of sense.

"Is Cam in trouble?" I ask, looking at Dimples.

"No, he's not in trouble. We're trying to sort out the whole story," he says.

"Right," I say. Sure. His dimples aren't fooling me. Not at all. We're all in trouble.

A minute later the talking dies down and the door opens. Cam is sitting quiet in the chair; he's slumped over now like a boxer after a big match.

"Izzy and Lucy, why don't you guys come in," Ms. Linda says. "Cam, you can go wait with Officer Doogan."

I look back at Dimples—Officer Doogan—and he smiles and gestures to the chair in the hallway. Cam gets up, focusing on the floor. I leave PingPing with Cam and we go with Ms. Linda and the other police officer. I'm getting tired of this already.

"You can sit," Ms. Linda says, taking her seat on the other side of the desk. Izzy gets into one of the chairs and I sit down in the other.

"What happened with Cam?" I say. "What's going on?"

"We've arranged for Camrin's parents to come pick him up," Ms. Linda says, smiling like she had some sort of victory.

"You mean his mom?" I say. "Not parents."

Ms. Linda nods. "Yes, Mrs. McKinney is on her way to pick Cam up."

This little family consultation room is really losing its cheery name. I look from one rosy wall to another.

"So." Ms. Linda puts her hands together on the desk. "We've arranged for Cam to go back to his family." I think about the radio broadcasts.

"Do they understand he wasn't kidnapped?" I ask. Izzy squirms in her seat next to me.

"I'm not at liberty to discuss Camrin's situation at the present, but I can assure you that we will be evaluating everything fully."

I can't help but let out a long sigh. Cam and me have the same situation. We're best friends, after all. But before I can tell her this, the police officer steps forward. "Mr. McKinney did openly state that he left on his own accord, rest assured."

"Thanks," I say, as Ms. Linda gives him a glare and continues.

"Do you guys have any family you can go to?"

If we had someone other than Useless Mama, wouldn't we have told her by now? I roll my eyes. I nearly stretch them out of their sockets to make it clear. "No," I say. "That means foster sc—foster care, right?"

Ms. Linda's head tilts to one side. "Yes, are you apprehensive about that?"

"Can we stay together?" I say.

Ms. Linda picks up a piece of paper. "Yes. I've spoken with Mary Quinn at Vermont Youth Services and they have a fantastic foster care family you both can stay with, available right away."

"I want Mama," Izzy says to me. This time she's turned all the way to me and not to Ms. Linda at all. She's getting wise to her maybe.

"There's nothing to be afraid of, Isabelle," Ms. Linda says. "I can understand how this is a frightening experience for you. But, your mother needs some medical attention."

That's for sure. Izzy places her thumb in her mouth and sits back down, facing the desk.

"Once she is med compliant and deemed competent, she'll be evaluated with the goal of reintegration into family life."

Izzy looks from Ms. Linda to me.

"She doesn't understand the words you're using," I say. I turn to Izzy. "They mean Mama is crazy and she needs to stay in a hospital until she's better. And if they think she can handle being a mom, which she probably can't, then we might be able to see her again."

I see Izzy's eyes fill with tears. My stomach turns.

"Cam's going to go back to his mom and D-Wayne and we're going to go with strangers." I notice my fingernails digging into the palm of my hand and I see the officer adjust his stance, probably in case he has to chase me down or something.

Ms. Linda rolls her lips together and apart. And I see a big gobby tear slide down Izzy's cheek.

"I want to see Mama," she huffs.

"Oh, c'mon, Izzy, we'll be better off anyway," I say, turning from her sad face to look at the flowers in the picture behind Ms. Linda. They're a light yellow, and I stare into them, wishing I was that painting. Sitting on the wall, just watching, not feeling a single thing.

"How about this," Ms. Linda says. She gets up and goes around her chair. She pulls a jacket off the back. It's the first time I see it there. It's Mama's oversized one. "I'll talk to the doctors and we'll figure out the right time for you to visit." She brings Mama's jacket around and drapes it over Izzy's shoulders. It swallows her up in its folds.

"Right now she's been deemed—she needs rest. She'll be going to the psychiatric ward, where she can get all the care she needs," Ms. Linda says.

The jacket crinkles as Izzy's shoulders shudder. Ms. Linda stands up and pulls the tissue box off the desk, holding it out. Izzy takes one, and as she moves, the jacket crinkles again. She reaches her hand into one of the pockets and pulls something out of it.

It's Mama's notebook. Still covered in tinfoil, pieces of paper sticking out around the edges. Izzy pulls out an envelope from between its pages. It has one of those clear plastic windows in the front of it. A bill, probably. But Izzy holds it out to me and familiar colors and big chunky letters decorate the corner of the envelope. I look closer. *Bot-Block Jr.* it says. My stomach twists. And in my head my Mission Control voice warns me, *spacecraft unstable. Emergency protocol initiated.* I wobble up and take the envelope from Izzy.

"What's this?" I say, holding it out in front of me.

I see Mama at the kitchen table on my birthday. I see her put the envelope in her journal. My throat burns. It can't be. I run my fingers over the address window.

> LUCILLE PEEVEY
> C/O MARGARET PEEVEY
> 43 SUNNYSIDE LANE
> CAMDEN, VT 05653

I flip it over. The letter has been opened. I brush the torn paper and lift the seal, sliding the letter out of the envelope. I unfold it, my eyes blurring. I can barely read it.

Thank you for registering for BotBlock Jr. in the junkbot division.

I breathe in sharply and the letters dance. Words and images fill my ears. Mama saying that a letter was important. I grab on to the desk, trying to steady my vision, but the whole place dips and twirls.

"Hold on!" the police officer says, rushing over to me.

"My birthday," I breathe as I slip to the side. I reach for him.

"I need help in here!" Ms. Linda shouts, rushing toward the door.

"It was Mama," I say. Mama. Running footsteps shake the paintings on the walls, and the officer's and Izzy's and Ms. Linda's faces swirl as I dip into darkness.

My eleventh birthday. We'd packed up all our bags to go to Seahook, but as we were loading the car, Gram started breathing heavy and sweating. We called 911 right away and they came and brought her to the hospital. A day later, instead of being surrounded by the sand and the stars, we were surrounded by a sea of tiles and fluorescents and monitors that tell everyone in the room if you are living or you are dying.

I held Gram's crinkled hand. She squeezed it every time she inhaled. I didn't like the tube snaking into her nose. I didn't like the smell of the hospital. I didn't like anything about it at all. I didn't like her eyes drooping or the trouble she was having talking. She went out of consciousness and back in. We went to the cafeteria and back out. And the doctors said critical, then recuperating, then critical. She floated away, then back to the surface and away again. Once when she was sort of together she asked for me. I went inside.

"I want to say a proper good-bye to . . . you . . ." She spoke like she had been running all her life. "While I have my senses with me."

"You'll be all right, won't you, Gram?" I choked, clutching her fingers. She didn't answer, but when I lifted my eyes

to hers, she had a grin in them. A twinkle shining out at me, saying "that's a funny joke, kid."

She took a deep breath and said, "I want you to remember one thing . . . If there is nothing else you remember—"

"I'll remember everything about you, Gram," I said.

"But if there is only one . . ." She paused and her throat wobbled. "Remember that you can do whatever you set your mind to . . . make a plan . . ."

I thought about Sunnyside. I thought about what it would be like without Gram.

"Take care of each other . . ."

"Don't go, Gram." The cold air in the hospital wrapped around my shoulders and shook them with its icy grip.

"Promise me." Gram's fingers tightened on my hand. "Lucy, promise me you'll take care of them. However you can. You're all they'll have left. Promise me if your mama gets lost in herself, you'll take control, okay?"

I tried to promise, but my throat wrapped too tight around my voice. Why couldn't we all just go home. All of us. Eat sandwiches and chips? Go to the beach? But when I finally lifted my eyes to Gram's, I could see that wasn't going to happen.

"Promise me," she said again.

"I promise," I choked, wondering if I even knew how to do what she was asking.

"You're a smart girl, Lucy, just like your mama. You're going to do something great. I know you will."

Gram erupted into a coughing fit.

The nurses and doctors came in, pushing me up and out of there, and I stayed in the waiting room the rest of the time, holding on to Izzy. Mama went out and then in, over and over. The last time she came out, she held Gram's sweater. I took the soft fabric between my fingers and looked at her for answers. But her eyes were blind to me. We were further apart than we'd ever been before.

Thirty-Five

THE FEELING OF THE SWEATER BETWEEN my fingers dissolves into a rough sheet and I blink my eyes open.

Beeeeeebabeep.

Beeeeeebabeep.

The monitor and the distinct sounds of the Cartoon Network fill my ears. I'm in a hospital bed now, an IV in the top of my right hand. I look down to see Izzy lying in the crook of one of my arms, watching the screen on the opposite wall. Cam and Ms. Linda are sitting in chairs underneath the TV monitor. Cam is looking toward the ocean. I follow his gaze out the window. It's getting to be sunset again. I squeeze Izzy's hand and she looks up at me.

"Hey," I whisper. "How long was I out?"

"Just a little while," Izzy says, hugging me tight. I try to sit up.

"Take it easy," Ms. Linda says, getting out of her chair. "You have gone through a great deal of trauma."

But I don't want rest. Not now.

"Where's my mama?" I ask Ms. Linda as she steps toward the door.

"Nurse!" she calls. The nurse comes down the hall and she and Ms. Linda start talking about something. Linda gestures toward me and speaks in a low voice.

Cam gets up from the chair on the opposite wall and comes over, climbing onto the end of the bed. He places Mama's journal down on my lap.

"Thought you might like that," he says.

I pick it up and flip through the pages. I flip from oldest to most recent, looking at the dates and headings. Sometimes they're there, sometimes they're not. Sometimes her writing is neat and organized, sometimes it is sloppy and fast.

January 24th
The winter feels longer than ever this year. Thought of Mom today. Think of her every day. It's like the snow. The missing is here to stay.

I flip to the next page. It's about Robert Frost. Then to the next.

February 28th
Lucy is working on a robot. The summers at Seahook with Mom really mean something to her. She and Cam, from next door, have written down all of their plans in a notebook. Sounds like

233

something that would be a good birthday surprise. Something I know she would like. No money for it, though.

I flip the page and scan.

I looked into it. Birthday surprise would only be three hundred sixty dollars. Think I can find a way to get her the money. Have been feeling a little numbed out, anyway. Dr. Vincent said we could maybe lower the lithium, but that doesn't exactly add up. I could wean myself off of the antipsychotic and save more quickly. Who wants to be on meds forever, anyway? There is a time to face reality, you know? Even if the sadness comes again for a while.

. . . Did it ever really leave?

My throat starts to close in on itself, wondering what is coming next, but thinking I already know the answer. Thinking I already know how this ends.

April 1st
Day one off clozapine, lithium, and Celexa. I have been taking half a dose of each for a month and it's going great.

Now they're all gone, but I filled the bottle with beans. Rattles all the same. :)

April 5th
Still thinking of Mom every day. In a way she's here with us. I sense her presence in all the quiet corners.

April 6th
Feeling great today. Forgot what it was like to feel so alive.

April 12th
Everything seems so much clearer to me now. The grass is brighter. I'm connected to everything. Have been doing a lot, feeling really productive. Almost ready to register Lucy for the BotBlock Challenge! Also making new work plans. We'll be out of Sunnyside and back on our feet before we know it.

How many months of missed medication would be enough to pay the registration?

May 1st
I know I should go back on my medication, but I just feel so much more

alive without it. My writing is back. I can feel the muse. I'm onto some fantastic ideas. Universal energy has favored me.

I flip the page so fast that it gets a little tear in the corner.

May 15th
Yesterday I could swear I was Robert Frost reincarnated. I know that sounds silly, of course. I mean my imagination got away with me for a moment. It was like I was him. Having the words flow from my pen.

The nurse is next to me and she puts a squeezy device on my arm.

May?
Feeling foggy today. Forgot my appointment twice. Have a lot to do. Starting with the oleander seeds.
Oleander seeds the breaded deeds
Watched the clock that supersedes
Bringing forth the mighty fight
That rang through hills dark nights
A one-in-a-million idea only comes

around once. What if someone else catches it out of the stratosphere? Someone would steal your words. Happens all the time. Have to be very careful of them

I look up at Cam.

"She went off her medication to pay for the BotBlock registration."

He nods.

"Then lost it." I close the book.

Izzy moves to the bottom of the bed next to Cam as the nurse puts the stethoscope in her ears and places it in the crook of my arm.

"Do they know?" I say, nodding toward Ms. Linda, who comes back into the room with a cup of coffee in her hand.

"I tried to explain," he says.

"Listen," I say, looking around the nurse's head, as she leans to look at the gauge pressed against my arm. "This is a big misunderstanding."

Something pinches as I shift, and I notice the IV needle in the back of my hand. I pull it out. The nurse's eyes go wide.

"Hold on, now, you can't do that." She pulls the stethoscope from her ears and takes hold of my hand. I stay still for just a second as she pushes the plastic into a little tube. It stings the teensiest bit and I pull my hand away.

"You need to let us go see Mama," I say.

Izzy jumps off the bed.

"You have to stay hooked up," Ms. Linda says. "Sit back and relax, please."

How can I possibly relax? Mama sacrificed her health for me and I screamed at her and left her. I called her crazy. I called her a waste.

"I need to talk to the officer. It's all a big mistake—"

"Lucille, your mother took someone else's child across state lines, stole an RV, and ran from the law. The police are looking into it, but we're looking at kidnapping." She gestures to Cam.

"For the last time, I ran away, I wasn't kidnapped," Cam says, getting up off the bed. He crosses his arms. "Mom knew I was going. I told her a thousand times and it's not my fault she doesn't pay any attention."

Ms. Linda raises her eyebrows, and I see her eyes drift to the bump and bruises on my arm from where I hit the couch. "There's also possible child abuse and neglect."

My heart starts to kick my chest, hits the back of my ribs. This isn't right.

"She didn't hit me. I fell. Anyway, she wasn't herself," I say. "She didn't have her medication."

Ms. Linda closes her hands together and takes a deep breath in. "There are policies and procedures to take care of this sort of situation. If your mother is deemed incompetent at the time of these incidents, then that will be taken under consideration and the charges may be dropped. I'm not saying they will or they won't be. But right now, the most important thing is for you, your sister, and Camrin to get to a safe place and heal."

"Yes, I know. You already said that!" My chest constricts. Ms. Linda must see me flinch.

"Please rest. You need time to come to terms with what has happened," the nurse says, adjusting my pillow.

"I know what happened!" I say. "I know exactly what happened. I don't need rest."

The pillow isn't fitting right behind me and I flatten down on it hard. The nurse looks at Ms. Linda like I smacked her across the face instead of sat back.

Ms. Linda comes around to stand next to the nurse. "I fully understand your pain, here, Lucille, but unfortunately, you have no choice in the matter. How about this—"

I feel my jaw tightening and my teeth pressing together so hard they might crack. I rub my hands over my face.

"—I'll speak with the psychiatric ward and see about a good time for you to talk to your mother. I'll see if we can get a date range so that you will feel better about this. How does that sound."

A date range? Weeks? Months? I pull the covers off my lap. I don't need a date to see my mama.

"I want to see her now."

"Sit back, please," the nurse says, pulling a cart to her side.

"Get out of my way," I say, scooting to the edge of the bed.

"Absolutely not," she says. "Please listen, you need to sit down."

"Lucille," Ms. Linda says. Officer Doogan appears in the doorway and I can see he's coming to detain me just like they did to Mama. Even without the blankets it's too hot. I have fireworks going off in my brain.

I try to stand up and the nurse comes toward me. I push at her and then the officer is there holding me back. I kick out, but the nurse quickly switches something in the needle in my hand and all of a sudden, I don't have use of my muscles anymore. I see Cam jump at Officer Doogan, who turns and puts his hand on Cam's shoulder. Here's my chance, but as I try to rise up again, the fireworks start to fade away, and I relax down even though I'm trying to go up. Izzy starts to scream. I see her mouth open, but her voice is low like it is coming through a conch shell. I drop back. Out of fuel. Ms. Linda's face waffles in front of me and I see her brow coming together into a long, wobbly line. Her lips move but her voice is so low and slow I can't make out what she is saying. I feel like I'm filling up with cotton. I want to tell them that they need to let me up, but when I try my tongue gets fat in my mouth. Everything is soft and foggy and slow. And then gone.

Thirty-Six

THE TILES AND THE SMELLS OF the hospital trick me into believing that I'm back with Gram. Making promises I can't keep. But as soon as I notice I'm the one in the bed, everything tumbles back to me. I wonder if Gram knows how hard I tried. If she's disappointed in me just the same.

I glance around the room. Cam and Izzy are curled up in the empty bed beside me. I'm not surprised Mrs. McKinney isn't here yet. I'll be surprised if she shows up at all. Ms. Linda is sound asleep across the room. Her head lolled back, neck out.

I look at the light of the fluorescent streetlamps, spilling into the black and blue hospital room. I hear the sound of the ocean. A steady hum in the distance.

"You're back?" Cam says real quiet. So quiet it fades into the roll of the waves and I wonder if I'm imagining things. I turn toward the bed on the other side and he climbs out as quiet as he can.

"I overheard a doctor saying they're waiting for a bed to open up in psych for your mom," Cam says.

The darkness seems to wrap around my shoulders and

arms. It's got weight and it's pushing down on me from every angle.

"The psych ward," I say. "Basically the same as Kensington."

Cam crosses his arms and leans them onto the bed rail. "Yeah. A lot of us going to places we don't want to go," he says.

"Yeah," I say, running my fingers along the edge of the blanket.

"Mission not accomplished," Cam says.

I put my hand on his shoulder, breathing deep. "I'm so sorry, Cam," I say. "To get you wrapped up in this stupid g—"

He pushes my hand off. "You can't always take all the credit, Juniper Ray. You know I wanted to be here."

It's dark out the window and I instinctively look to my watch, but it's not there. "What time is it?"

"About three thirty in the morning," he says. "My mom is late, go figure." I hear his voice constrict.

"That's okay. At least we're all still together."

"For the moment," he says.

I sit back feeling the defeat slip in. I see us out in deep space. Me, Mama, Izzy, and Cam in our astronaut suits. No pilot and no ship. Just floating away from each other into the endless universe. Cam climbs onto the bed, pressing his back up against the bar at the bottom. He folds his hands together and we sit quietly for a minute. I feel a tickle at my armpit and when I reach to scratch it, my fingertips find the foil wrapped around Mama's journal. I pull it out and think about how Mama clutches it. How she scribbles all her thoughts and worries and new ideas into it.

"It wasn't all bad," Cam says.

I look up to see his eyes fade into memory. "The way D-Wayne screamed when I put that bike helmet on my head."

For a second I'm back at Sunnyside. A blaze of dust flying out behind us as we made our exit. "The way we flew out of that carport and Chuck ran alongside," I say.

"I was hoping he would make it." Cam grins.

"The look on Mr. Blinks's face. Like he never saw anything so good in his whole life. Thinking we were going to make our own destiny," I say, fiddling with the tube that's reaching down into the back of my hand.

Tears burn my eyes and I think of Mama. I look from Ms. Linda, dozing in the chair, over to Izzy on the bed, to Cam, and then outside. The moon hangs there, heavy in the arms of the sky. It soaks the world beyond the window in blue. And off in the distance, I can see the Milky Way, and below it, a beach filled with the glowing blue moon shells. I push myself up and as I do, Mama's journal tumbles from my hand. A long slip of paper slides out onto the sheet. I pick it up. Run my hand along a rough edge. I see the lettering at the top: *Acquainted with the Night*.

"It's that poem that Mama's been stuck on," I say, seeing her take it out of the anthology. It's creased and worn and faded in spots, like it has soaked up a lot of tears. And I wonder if she'd feel better telling it to the moon. I think of her journal, the most important thing to her besides us. Just like our Mission Control notebook. Plans of a different kind. My insides twinge together, like my wires are running to all the wrong places.

I pull the IV from my hand.

Cam looks up at me "Wha—"

I shake my head and put my index finger to my mouth. "We have to go find Mama. I want to bring her journal to her. She'll feel better if she has it," I say.

Cam points to Ms. Linda. "We're still going to have to sneak out without her noticing," he hisses. "We'll need some sort of distraction."

All of a sudden there's a clatter in the hallway and Ms. Linda's head snaps up. I drop onto the pillow, pretending sleep. Then I yawn and raise my arms in the air. Cam gets it right away because he jumps in.

"How'd you sleep?"

I stretch. "Pretty good," I say, looking at him. But just then I see his face freeze like a squirrel when a big dog is nearby. I follow his gaze out to the hallway. There, through the window, is the ugliest thing on the planet: D-Wayne.

Thirty-Seven

"SIR, EXCUSE ME, MAY I HELP you?" Officer Doogan says, hands up, palms out.

"I've come to get the boy." D-Wayne stares over Officer Doogan's shoulder at us. And he's chewing on something, his jaw jiggling up and down with the effort. Ms. Linda gets up out of her chair and pulls her glasses onto her face.

"Figures," Cam says, sliding off the bed, onto his feet. Not to go to him, I imagine, but to get ready for some sprinting.

"You're not Mrs. McKinney," Ms. Linda says, striding across the floor.

"They must pay you the big bucks." D-Wayne smirks and rubs the unshaven hair on his chin.

"I'm sorry, are you Camrin's father?" Ms. Linda asks, not missing a beat.

"No, he's not," Cam says. Ms. Linda spins toward us and then back toward D-Wayne. She blocks the doorway.

"I'm close enough," D-Wayne says. "Aren't I, boy?" He winks at Cam over Ms. Linda's shoulder.

Cam crosses his arms. "I don't think so," he says.

D-Wayne steps toward Officer Doogan, but Ms. Linda puts her hand between them.

"I'm sorry, but unless you have identification showing that you're one of Mr. McKinney's relations, you're going to have to leave."

"Well, excuuuuse me," D-Wayne says. His gaze goes from Ms. Linda's feet to her head as he says it. I don't have to see her face to know she doesn't like that one bit.

"Ehem, well." She leans back and grabs the door handle. "If you'll excuse us for a moment." She pulls the door shut behind her. Just like that, we're all alone in the hospital room. And I'm starting to like Ms. Linda a whole lot more. Their voices rise and a second later, I see them walk past the window and around the corner.

"For once maybe something he's doing will work out for us," Cam says, jumping up and down.

I slide out from under the covers. Take Mama's journal and tuck it into the front of my pants.

"We don't have a plan," Cam says. "We don't even know where your mama is."

"Fifteen-B," Izzy says.

"Huh?" I say, my head snapping up. Is she talking in her sleep?

"She's in fifteen-B," Izzy says again. I see her hand grab the railing and she rises up from the covers like a little mole from its den. She rights the wire crown on her head.

"Izzy, how do you know that. Did you see her?" I ask, rushing over to her side and grabbing her shoulders.

"No, I heard Ms. Linda asking the man in the white coat if we could see Mama and he said, 'No, no, they cannot. She needs to go to psych.' And then Ms Linda said, 'It's really important. Are you sure she isn't okay to see them.' And then he said, "'Scuse me, Mrs. Burningham, but if you're more qualified to assess Mrs. Peevey, then by all means go down to fifteen-B and dig nose yourself.'"

"Diagnose?" I say.

Izzy nods. "Something like that. His face got pretty red."

I give her a squeeze.

"Now, we just need to know where fifteen-B is."

"Got it," Cam says. I help Izzy down. We walk over to where Cam is standing. He's tracing his finger over something on the wall.

"Emergency procedures floor plan."

My mouth goes dry.

"We need to go right down this hallway, take one right, next left, then find the number."

"Let's go," I say, grabbing Izzy's hand. "We gotta sneak." We go to the door. PingPing sits in the corner where Officer Doogan left him and he looks out at me with his LED eyes. His football head looks a little bit more crushed than usual. He's been having a heck of a journey.

"We gotta go now if we're going," Cam says, sliding the door open. He looks both ways, then ducks his head back in. He sees me looking at PingPing. "What are you thinking, Cap'n?"

"I think we might need him," I say. I rush to the corner and pick PingPing up. "Let's go."

And just like that, we sneak out into the hallway, silent as can be. I hear Officer Doogan and Ms. Linda talking in short sentences around the corner. Cam grabs my shoulder and we head in the opposite direction. Toward the east wing.

Thirty-Eight

"Mighty Hawk, this is Juniper Ray," I hiss. "We got nurses at two o'clock."

"Security at four o'clock," Cam says as we duck into a bathroom. Cam reaches up and spins the lock to the right. It latches.

"This is crazy, right?" I say, hunkering down and setting PingPing on the floor for a second.

"Yeah, delusional," Cam says, smiling.

Izzy presses her ear up against the door and I lean in, too, waiting for the footsteps to disappear down the hall.

"So if we're right"—Cam stands up and looks at the blueprint attached to the bathroom wall—"she's right around the corner. She should be two doors down."

Could it be that easy? I grab the handle, unlatch the lock, and slide the door open a tiny crack. I peer out.

"It's clear," I say. I look at Izzy and put my finger up to my lips. "Quiet as can be, okay? Just like when Queen Nomony had to sneak in to free the Tinktree people."

She puts her finger up to her mouth, mirroring me. I lift PingPing again and we slip into the hallway and along the wall. I stop at the corner. Clear one way. I stick my head out and peer to the right. There's a lady sitting right at the table next to a door. I jump back. Squeeze against the wall. I shake my head at Cam. Then hold my hand out, take a breath, and look again. She's in a chair next to a room marked 15B Observation. She starts to turn her head our way and I wave my hands at Cam. We scramble back down the hall.

"Not clear," I mouth.

"In here," Cam says, sliding a door open. We duck inside, but Izzy and I get tangled and we trip into the room. I stumble forward, keeping PingPing up off the floor until the last second. Mama's journal jams itself into my rib cage. I come down a twisted heap and set PingPing down the rest of the way. Cam and Izzy grab my arms and start helping me up. Just as I am getting back to my feet a little old lady sits up in the bed in front of us. My heart bangs against my chest as I scramble. She looks from me to Izzy to Cam.

"Please?" I say. Pressing a finger to my mouth. Her eyes slide sideways. Then she leans back against her pillow, sucking one cheek in.

"Looks like trouble to me," she mutters. "I've been in a fair bit of trouble in my day." Then just like that she flicks the TV on and starts flipping the channels, acting like we're not there.

"Thank you," I whisper, but she doesn't seem to hear me. Instead, she reaches her hand out and pulls a curtain around the edge of her bed. She gives me a wink and disappears behind the cloth.

"Don't send them to me when you get caught, though," I hear her say.

I get up high enough so I can peer between the blinds on the window. If I angle just right I can see down the next hallway. Not very well, though. I can't see the lady or the door to the room. All I can see is the corner of her elbow, which appears and disappears from sight.

"Someone's watching Mama," I say.

Izzy gets up on her tippy toes to peer out and Cam leans in.

"Is it a cop? I can't see," he says.

"No, it's not a cop. I don't think." I picture the lady sitting there. "She was reading a book. I don't think she's a nurse, either."

"Not wearing a blue outfit like the rest of them?" Cam asks. He lets go of the blinds.

"Nope. I think she was wearing jeans and a T-shirt."

"Hrm." This was not in the plan. Though we didn't really have one to begin with. Izzy slides PingPing over to the wall and starts talking to him under her breath.

"Don't be afraid, soldier," she says, holding on to the sides of his arms.

"We need to lure her away from that door," Cam says. I hear footsteps coming down the hallway. I peer out to see a nurse walking toward the nurse's station.

"Get down," I hiss. We slide down next to Izzy, leaning our backs up against the wall. PingPing seems to look at me, telling me he can do it, if I let him. I glance at Cam and back at PingPing.

"You're kidding me, right?" Cam says, reading my thoughts.

"Kidding what?" Izzy says, looking confused.

"It's the only way," I tell him.

The footsteps draw closer and I hold my breath. Then they recede and disappear down the hall.

"Okay," Cam says.

"Okay," I say.

"Okay what?" Izzy asks.

I pull the remote control from its spot around Ping-Ping's neck. "Sorry, Izzy. PingPing's moment of glory has finally come."

"Huh?" She stands up. "Where's he going?"

"He's going for a ride," Cam explains, moving toward the door. He opens it a crack, kneels, and looks down the hallway. Izzy gives PingPing a hug. I pat him on the head, trying to tell myself we'll see him on the other side, but I'm not one hundred percent sure that that's true.

"Be brave," Izzy says, looking into his LED eyes.

"We have a nurse's cart on the right," Cam says. "If we can crash him into it, it may draw her away." I move my hand from PingPing's head, make sure that Izzy isn't looking into his eyes, and flip on his power switch. He makes a little *wuw-whir, wuw-whir*. The TV that the old lady is watching gets louder. I smile. Nice to have someone on our side for once.

I wrap the RC lanyard around my neck and pull out the antenna. Cam comes over to me and picks up PingPing. Then he grabs the door handle and sets PingPing down next to him.

"Is it clear the other way?" Cam asks as he opens the door a crack. Izzy stands up on her tippy toes and looks through the window toward Mama's room.

"Clear this way," she says. "Except for the guard." Cam opens the door a little more. Just wide enough for PingPing to get out. I take a breath and put my thumb on the joystick.

"On your go, Cap'n," Cam says, letting go of PingPing. My right thumb fires the joystick forward, then to the right as I steer him out the door. Cam slides it mostly closed and I go over so I can see PingPing racing down the hall to the nurse's cart.

I toggle the joystick, touching lightly left and right until he is barreling toward the nurse's station straight ahead.

"Collision course is acquired," Cam says. "Impact in five, four, three, two."

One flick with my left thumb and I lift PingPing's hands. They shoot straight up.

"One," Cam says. A loud crash sounds as PingPing collides with the cart; his upturned hand gets caught on a loose bedpan and the next second I flip my left thumb again and he wings it into the air. It comes crashing down, collides with the tiles, and spins. *Ka-ping-wing-wing-wing*. I keep my right thumb pressed forward and PingPing glances off of the station, running it into the wall again and again. It becomes unsteady and sheets, a stethoscope, and some other metal tools skitter to the floor with every jostle.

"She's on the move," Izzy says, letting go of the blinds. I watch as another piece of metal falls and slides under PingPing, *clinkclank*. The metal detector goes off.

Pling-tink, pling-tink, pling-tink.

I see a few heads pop out of the doors beyond the cart. Then footsteps sound and the guard passes us, the soles of her sneakers flashing quickly like warning lights.

"Please return to your rooms," she tells everyone. "Nothing to see here." Though it sounds like she isn't quite sure herself.

"Let's go," Cam hisses. "We don't have much time." He shifts his weight and slides the door open. I flip the remote control off and grab for Izzy's hand. We sneak low and quiet out the door and past the desk. *Room 15B, Observation*. I place my hand on the door handle, turn it, and step inside.

Thirty-Nine

MAMA. SHE'S LYING ON HER SIDE facing away from the door, and all I can see are her big black curls cascading down her back. Her silver streaks seem dull, almost nonexistent here in the shadows.

Her voice tickles the darkness. "I don't want to go, now why are you doing that?" Quiet words.

I crush my eyelids closed. My throat is filled with stardust, jagged edges, dark matter. Something inside me cracks open.

"Mama?" I say real quiet. She breathes in sharply and tries to flip over.

"It's okay, it's okay," I say, coming around the side of her bed. I can see her in the light spilling in the window. Her eyes are wide and rimmed with tears.

"Lucy?" Her voice has a low timbre to it, like she has been crying forever. Sharp-edged tears rubbing her throat raw.

Izzy comes over to me, and Cam stands watch at the door, peering out between the blinds, his head turning back and forth and back and forth.

"My girls," Mama says.

I reach my hand into hers. And I look at my mama. My mama, who remembered my birthday. My mama, who took the biggest risk she could possibly take. My mama, who is chaos walking. My mama, trying the best she can. Same as me. My mama, full of love. She looks so sad, bruised and broken. And I look from her to Cam to Izzy. We all have our heads in the sand. Like that's all we've known for a long, long time. Like that's all we'll know for a long time to come. Gram's voice rings in my ears. *One second you're so high you can taste the sweetness of the Milky Way*. I want that. I want that for me, and Cam and Mama and Izzy. But we're not in any position to reach it. Not if others are going to make our decisions for us.

"You know," Mama says, "they're gonna numb out my brain."

Her pupils go in and out like a telescope lens trying to focus. I follow her gaze past my shoulder and out into the night. I go and slide the window open. It stops about an inch up. But I can hear the ocean. And a light breeze tickles my fingers, calling us on. When I turn back, Mama closes her eyes, and I can see the sounds of the ocean are soothing her. I look down to my waist, pull the journal from the front of my pants. I bring it to her and press it into her hand.

"Here's your notebook, Mama, and your poems."

Her eyes flutter open and she smiles at me, but once

again her gaze finds the sky over my shoulder. I look out at it, then over to Cam at his post by the door.

"Hey, Mighty Hawk, is it quiet out there?" I ask.

Cam leans toward the window and flicks the blinds apart with his index and middle finger. "Uh, negative, Juniper Ray. We have activity. A few patients out."

"Could we get to the elevator?" I ask, hearing a lone seagull behind me.

Cam looks across the room at me, finally seeing what I'm getting at. A smile finds its way to one side of his lips. He nods. "Oh yeah, I'm sure of that. Nothing's impossible. If we want it bad enough."

Izzy reaches up and squeezes my free hand.

"You want to go for a midnight ride, Mama?" I look at her, wondering if she understands me. Wondering if she can hear me through the fuzz. If she knows I'm here or if she's just talking to the world. I get down so that I can look her right in the eyes.

"A midnight ride?" I say. "You wanna go?"

And I don't know if I'm imagining it, but I swear that underneath the dark and dust, her eyes get a glimmer.

I wrap Mama in her blanket. As I tuck it in, she rolls up into a sitting position. I fold it around her shoulders and pull it over her back, so it's in a spiral around her. She grasps it at her shoulders, holding it in place.

"Mighty Hawk, if you don't want to be part of this, I totally understand," I whisper.

"And let you have all the fun? Get off your high horse, Juniper Ray," he says. He goes to the bed on the other side of the room, pulls the blanket from it, and fashions himself a cape. "You need me."

"You're darn right I do," I say as I pick up Izzy and put her on the edge of the bed.

"Mama," she says, leaning forward. "You okay, Mama?" Mama reaches her blanketed arms out and Izzy finds a spot in between them, wrapped in a hug.

I hear Cam suck in a breath.

"We got a nurse at three o'clock." He points to the right. I rush over to the window. We watch as she starts down the hallway, opening doors and peering in.

"We better go now," I say.

I hurry to Mama's bed and flip the brake.

"We're going for a ride?" Izzy says.

"Yeah. You hang on tight," I say, feeling like I'm a rocket ship getting ready for launch. I flex my feet, angle the bed. Cam takes a deep breath. "Juniper Ray?" Cam hisses. "This is Mighty Hawk."

I hear a few voices in the hallway. I don't know where they are, but either way, we're getting ready to get out of here, so they best clear out.

"We got takeoff in five . . ."

I push forward slightly. Izzy claps her hands and Mama grips the bed railing with one hand.

"Four . . ." Cam inches the door open a tiny bit. I hear voices in the hallway. Footsteps.

"Three . . ." He goes silent and let's his fingers do the counting. *Two*. I lean forward. *One*. He tears the door open and we spill into the hallway.

We're on our way. Moving, running.

Chasing the Milky Way.

Forty

WE SAIL DOWN THE HALL, WHEELS sliding and squeaking as we make the turn toward the elevator. Cam gets out in front, skids toward the doors, and slams the button hard. I slide my feet to a halt in front of it.

"Hurry, hurry, hurry," I say. Cam's fingers match my words, hitting the down arrow over and over again.

"There they are!" I hear to my right. I glance down the hall. Yep, it's Ms. Linda and Officer Doogan at the far end.

"Stop right there!" Doogan says, but he's not pulling out his gun, so I figure we're good to go.

"What do you think you're doing?" Ms. Linda says. They both begin running toward us. The elevator chimes and I push hard, sliding in. Cam slams the door-close button. The footsteps thunder closer. The doors begin to slide closed. Slowly, so slowly, too slowly. I jump up and down.

"Stop!" I hear. "Security!"

Izzy shrieks, her hands going into the air. Then Doogan and Ms. Linda appear and then disappear as the doors slide shut. We begin to drop.

"And we have liftoff!" Cam shouts.

The elevator buttons light up as we reach floor 3, 2, 1,

lobby. I shake out my hands the whole way. And Izzy jabbers to Mama about our adventure. Mama holds on to Izzy and her journal, running her fingers over the foil.

"C'mon, c'mon, c'mon." I adjust the bed so I can angle it out the door. Just as I get the corner in line we jolt to a halt and the door dings and slides open.

A lady at the check-in looks over at us, her eyes begging for a distraction, and right away, I see why. It's D-Wayne, leaning up against her desk.

"Oh boy," I say. Cam jams himself between the bed and the door and D-Wayne turns. When he sees us, he stands up and his unshaven face spreads into a grin.

"My boy," he says. "You owe me money and a bike helmet, son!" He twirls a toothpick in his mouth. Cam rights himself, steps out into the lobby, and waves me on.

"Cam?" I say, as I swing the bed around to the right, toward a ramp that leads to the door. "What are you thinking?"

"What are you wearing?" I hear D-Wayne say.

"You go!" Cam shouts.

"You have to come, too!" I slide the bed to the top of the ramp

"I'll be right behind you!" Cam says. "I'm much faster than him, remember?"

"You're not going anywhere. It's time you come home to your ma," D-Wayne tells him.

One heave onto the ramp and we have gravity on our side. We pick up speed as we head for the sliding door.

Cam skips backward alongside me. Out of the corner of my eye, I see D-Wayne fly toward us. The lady at check-in is grabbing for the phone. We hit the bottom of the ramp and D-Wayne leverages himself over the railing with his hand. At the same time, Cam grabs a chair from the entryway, picks it up, and swings into motion. Then all I here is a crash and a "gogoGO!" and an "ooophhffff."

We sail out of the sliding door.

"You're going to pay for that!" D-Wayne says in a strained voice, but Cam is there beside me now, and we're gone. Onto the sidewalk. The ocean beats against the shore in the distance, calling us: *Runrunrunrun*.

"Warp speed, Cap'n!" Cam says. We move together as fast as we can. Mama's laugh bubbles up and it flies my heart toward the moon.

"Stop right where you are!" Ms. Linda shouts behind us. I hear her high heels clip along the sidewalk, then stagger. Cam grabs one side of the bed, and I grab the other and we push, shoulder to shoulder. Stride in stride. Down Ocean Avenue. I don't care who's after us. I don't care what happens next. All I want is now. This feeling. Running out in front of everyone. In control of our next steps and our last memories. We roll across an intersection. A car skids, slamming on its brakes. And we bob and careen up onto the sidewalk.

BEACH, a sign points north. I follow the arrow.

"Feel the breeze, Mama?!" I shout.

She raises her hands straight up into the air and Izzy's

mirror hers. Mama's dark curls blow out behind her as we slide into the sand. I push us as far as I can, but we sink and the bed rolls to a stop. I run around to the side, pick up Izzy, and lift her onto the ground. Mama holds on to her journal and I prop my shoulder underneath her arm and help her to her feet. Izzy runs and puts her toes in the water. Cam gets under Mama's other side and I look to the water and the stars. Walk toward the Milky Way, stepping over moon shells. The wind beats off the ocean. Tugs at our shoulders. Tells us there is a heartbeat beyond our skin. Me and Mama and Cam. Izzy's running like a little girl should, blasting the waves into pieces.

I hear the crinkle of foil and see Mama looking down at her hand, at the journal she's been holding. Like she's finding it for the first time in a long time. A crinkled scrap flits in the wind, and she pulls it from between the pages. I see her trying to recollect what it is.

"It's Robert Frost, Mama, you love him, remember?" I say. I lean into her and we look at the poem together. "Remember? You love reading poetry to the moon. 'I have been one acquainted with the night'?"

The breeze licks the page, but I can still read the words.

I have walked out in rain—and back in rain.
I have outwalked the furthest city light.

Mama looks up from the paper, to me. Questions in her eyes. And I wonder if she gets it. If she sees I have a debt to repay. A promise I'm still doing my best to keep. She curls her fingers over the blanket, hugging it around her, then she spreads it out, like wings. And we huddle. Izzy runs in from the water and we curl together, the blanket flapping around us.

"'I have looked down the saddest city lane,'" Mama says, tilting her cheek onto my head. She knows this poem by heart.

A tear slips from her eye and rolls down her cheek. I feel it flit against my forehead.

> *I have passed by the watchman on his beat*
> *And dropped my eyes, unwilling to explain.*

I hear the footsteps thunder their way down the sidewalk to us. But I plant my feet in the sand and watch the waves roll into the bay. I raise my arms to the sky just like Mama does.

> *I have stood still and stopped the sound of feet*
> *When far away an interrupted cry*
> *Came over houses from another street,*

I peer over my left shoulder to see Ms. Linda and Officer Doogan in the sand. And Ms. Linda puts her hand on Doogan's arm.

"Give them a minute," she says quietly. "They're not going anywhere."

"That's true," Cam says, hearing her, too.

Mama's whispers flit out over the sound of ocean waves. "'But not to call me back or say good-bye.'"

I shout with her.

> *And further still at an unearthly height,*
> *One luminary clock against the sky*

And I watch the path along the surface of the water as it moves and shimmers. A landing strip to space. And I look up and see the Milky Way. A long dusty path that I'd like to skip down. The poem slips out of Mama's hand and skitters across the waves. Dips and twirls. And catches flight.

She sends it off with a shudder and a tear. "'Proclaimed the time was neither wrong nor right.'"

I look at Cam and Izzy and remember the last line, just like the first. *I have been one acquainted with the night.*

We stare up at the stars. The bright constellations. And when I look, I see tears on Mama's cheeks, and I see tears on Cam's cheeks, and I feel them drip down mine. But we're smiling, too.

The sirens sound and my hands find moon shells, right in front of me, blue-soaked edges. I pick one up and curl it into Mama's hand. Wanting, wanting so bad, to believe in the magic. She wraps her fist around it and we sit together in a heap. I breathe the fresh salt sea air. And I memorize this moment.

"They're coming for us, Juniper Ray," Cam says. He moves from Mama's other side over to mine and I wrap my arm around his waist. And we hold on. Because right here, we're perfect. Because for one more second, no one has us. For one more second, Cam is free, and Izzy and I aren't in the system, and Mama isn't in Kensington or the psych ward. For one more second, we're out in front, making the world wonder which way we're going to go. One more second, out of the black hole. One millisecond out of the void. Taking care of each other. Before the darkness comes for us all, I look up, taste the sweetness of the Milky Way, and surrender.

10 Months Later

I PUT MY SUITCASE DOWN AS we walk into the living room. It's our first night back at Sunnyside since we went to live with Mr. and Mrs. Benko. That's our foster mom and dad. They were really nice. I was surprised how nice. Mama has been here with her caseworker and I've been here with Izzy and mine. Between us, we got the trailer cleaned up pretty good. Mostly Mama did all the work. Izzy steps around me with the vase of flowers while I pull a loaf of bread from a paper bag and set it across the pretty checkered tablecloth that decorates the dining room table. Everything seems brighter in here now.

"I think Mama's going to like that," Izzy says.

I pull her in next to me. "Me too."

"Why don't you put your bags into your room and start unpacking," Mrs. Dockett says. Mrs. Dockett is our Vermont caseworker. She's sort of like Ms. Linda.

I walk through the living room. Past Mama's desk. Three Robert Frost books are in a neat pile. There are no stacks around our feet, just books lined up row upon row in the shelf. I think it would look real nice with one of the flowers perched on her desk, waiting for her arrival, so I usher Izzy on and return to the kitchen. I select one brown-eyed Susan.

"Can I put one of these on Mama's desk?" I ask as Mrs. Dockett looks at me out of the corner of her eye.

"I think that's a lovely idea," she says, pulling a glass from the cupboard. I take it from her and fill it with water. Then hurry back to the desk, put it on the upper right corner. It catches the sun, making a little yellow glow over the books and notebook.

I step into our bedroom. Izzy is sitting on the edge of her bed. I drop my suitcase on mine and start pulling out all my pants first. Cam's head pops up in the window. He grins from ear to ear. I scan his face from the top of his hairline to his shoulders and take a deep sigh of relief. Genuine smile. No bruises.

He pushes himself up on the window frame and executes a perfect somersault onto the bed. Then jumps up and wraps me in a hug.

"Never thought I'd say this, but it's good to have you back in Sunnyside." I feel his heart beat against my chest. I squeeze him extra hard.

"It's good to be back," I say.

"Is it true that D-Wayne is gone?" Izzy asks from behind us.

Cam pulls away from me and bounces back onto the bed. "Yeah, the court told Mom to lose him or lose us. He's court-ordered to stay away from here. And Mom's doing good, too. She even works an extra shift at the grocery now. And I got"—he reaches into his back pocket and digs out a card, holding it out to us—"this!"

"You got your YMCA membership?" I say, picking up a pile of clothes and sliding them into the bottom drawer of my dresser.

"Yeah, it's pretty great," he says, punching the air three times. "Coach Truman says I got a real knack."

"Of course you do," I say.

"I wanna go to the pool," Izzy says. I look over to see a small pile of crumpled clothes on her pillow.

"Try to put those in your drawers," I say. I pull out the bottom drawer of her dresser hoping it will prompt action.

Mrs. Dockett comes in, takes one look at Izzy's pile and tsk-tsks. She goes over to the pillow. Before she leans down to help she pauses like she is remembering something. She reaches into her bag and pulls out a bundle of envelopes.

"The mail," she says, handing it to me. I take it and drop it onto the bedcover. The envelopes cascade off the pillow onto the blanket. As it spills, I see one with the familiar BotBlock colors in the upper left-hand corner.

"You coming over for dinner?" I say to Cam, who has gone to the edge of the bed and is doing push-ups against the rail.

"You sure it's okay?" he asks, puffing between each pump.

I pull the envelope from the pile.

"Mama said she wanted you to come," I tell him.

"Then I'll be here." Cam grins.

I flip the envelope over and peel the top. Then I pull the letter out. I fold it open and scan the page.

Corporate Headquarters . . .

Your story . . .

We would like to count your registration toward next year's BotBlock competition . . .

Three categories of your choosing . . .

"Cam," I say, waving the letter. "Stop what you're doing and come look at this!"

He pushes himself off the edge of the bed and comes to look over my shoulder.

"They want us to compete this year," I say, showing him the letter.

He reads through. "Well, I guess we have some work to do. A new mission."

"That's right," I say. My mind starts working on the possibilities. I've been helping Mrs. Shareze run the robot club at school to pay her back for the laptops I lost and destroyed. I'm betting she might let me borrow one if I show her the letter. I start looking around the room for a pencil when I hear tires on the driveway.

I put the letter down on top of my suitcase and me and Cam and Izzy go through the living room and into the kitchen. Mrs. Dockett comes, too, but she hangs back just a bit. Mama walks in through the front door and I hold my breath. She looks from me to Izzy to Cam. Her eyes clear and shining. She kneels down.

"My, it's good to be here," she says, holding her arms out. We rush in for a hug. Dr. Vincent says that Mama is doing real well for the moment. It'll never be easy, but it may get easier as we go, as Mama learns more and more about what she needs to do to keep her illness at bay. To recognize the signs and symptoms.

"Who wants homemade macaroni and cheese?" Mama says.

"I do," Izzy shouts. Mama and Izzy pull the noodles from the cupboard and cheese from the fully stocked fridge.

Cam and I set the table. And we talk and catch up while we're at it. Mama said she nailed an interview with the University of Cleary in the Northeast Kingdom as tenure-track professor of English.

"So, we'll see," Mama says. "There's a lot to be said for keeping busy, challenging your mind."

As the sun starts to set, Sunnyside Trailer Park turns orange under the glow. Mrs. Dockett says good night. "I'll look forward to seeing all of you on Thursday." She opens the door.

"Four o'clock," Mama says, looking at the calendar. "We'll be there."

Mrs. Dockett closes the door and Mama pulls a steaming pan of mac and cheese from the oven. I dish up a scoop for each of us and Cam and I tell Mama about the Bot-Block Challenge. Mama looks a little nervous when we mention BotBlock, but then she relaxes as we talk more about what we might do for a design.

"Well, sounds like you kids have quite a project," Mama says as she and Cam clear the plates from the table. As the last dish goes into the strainer, I see Mama looks real tired.

"You should go in the living room and rest," I say.

Mama grabs a dish towel from the handle on the fridge and wipes her hands. "I may do a little bit of writing before bed."

"Is it Mission Control time?" Izzy asks, turning to me.

"Yeah, we could do that," I say. "That okay, Mama?"

"Of course it is," Mama says. The dish towel swings as she places it back around the handle of the fridge. "You kids go ahead."

We make our way through the door of the living room and Mama comes in, stopping as she sees the flower on the corner of her desk. With the setting sun, it's lit up like it's from another planet. Like it was picked from the red soil of Mars. Mama goes over to it and places her hands on her desk like she is greeting an old friend. I wonder, for just a second, if she is happier to see those dusty books than she is to see me and Izzy. But then I see her dig something out of her pocket. It's the moon shell I gave her. She sets it carefully next to the flower, angling it just right.

"Lucy? Can I talk to you for a second?" Mama says. I stop, but Cam ushers Izzy through our bedroom door and out the window.

"I . . ." Mama slides a drawer open on her desk and pulls out a card. "I wanted to give you this." She presses the card between her fingers. I recognize it. The card I found on my birthday night. "I know it's late, but—it got lost in the chaos."

I step toward her, take the card in my hand. I slide my finger underneath the seal.

I skip the Hallmark mumbo jumbo and go to Mama's real handwriting.

Happy birthday, baby girl. You're a miracle. I hope that 12 treats you well. I'll do everything I can to make sure it does. Gram would be so proud.
Love,
Mama

She reaches over and pushes a piece of hair behind my ear. She smells like vanilla. "I'm going to do the best I can. I want you to know I'm going to try very hard. I have a new plan." She pulls out her notebook. There isn't any foil on it. She opens it to a marked page and tears it out. Puts it on her corkboard near her desk. It's a checklist.

Reminders for Every Day

Time with Lucy and Izzy
Exercise
Write
Dr. Vincent
Critique Group
Medication
Tea with friends

"Dr. Vincent says a lot of it is about staying engaged."

It looks just like Mission Control. She checks off several of the reminders, then turns to me. She squeezes me tight. "I love you. That's the only thing that comes easy."

I lean in to her then. Mama, fully here. Just as she is, just as she should be. And I'm the happiest to have her back. We just stay, holding each other, like if one of us moves, the other will go crashing down.

"Lucy?" Izzy calls from the carport. Mama leans back and squeezes my shoulders with her hands. She gives me a kiss on the forehead.

"You go play. Have fun. Be a kid."

"Love you," I say, turning toward my door.

"Love you, too," she says.

I climb out the window and duck underneath the tarp

into the carport. It's more crooked than it was when we left. Resurrecting it wasn't too bad, though, since it's mostly just poles and plastic. Mr. Blinks had most of it back up by the time we arrived.

I meet Cam and Izzy over at the desk. Then I flick the light on and open the Mission Control notebook to the next empty page. I grab a fresh glue stick, run the glue across the paper, and paste the card down on it. Then I flip to the Protocol for Optimum Achievement. Look at the last two unfinished tasks on our list.

Go to BotBlock (and win)
Make dreams come true

The Mustang is no longer in the middle of the floor and Cam uses the space to kick and punch and swing. Izzy pulls a wire from a bucket and starts to fashion a crown. And I flip the page and rewrite those two goals up at the top.

"What are you doing, Cap'n?" Cam says as he comes over.

I turn the page toward him. "I'm reworking our protocol for optimum achievement." I hit the page with the eraser. "Just seems like a good place to start. Less obstacles this time. Less to do, means maybe we'll make it a little farther next time."

He reads it and then nods. "Yeah, it does. But it's not going to be easy."

I glance to the page and think about Mama's plan, too, and think maybe between all of us, we could make it happen. Maybe between all of us, we have a chance.

I raise my hand to my mouth like I'm holding up a walkie-talkie.

"Mighty Hawk, this is Captain Juniper Ray of the Vintage Carrier twenty-five, twenty-five."

Cam stands up straight, with soldier shoulders.

"Are you . . . afraid?" I say.

"I'm not afraid, Cap'n." Izzy comes over with her crown on and stands next to Cam.

"Fall in," I say, pulling PingPing from underneath the desk. I slide him next to Izzy.

"And if we're to fly out into the void and become live bait for aliens, will you be afraid?" I say, clasping my hands behind my back and walking to the right and then to the left.

"I will not be afraid, sir," Izzy says, giving me a sharp salute.

"And if we run out of fuel and have to walk through the stars until our feet bleed, will you be afraid?" I shout. Cam shakes his head.

"I will not know the name of fear, sir," Izzy shouts.

"And if we're taken down by space police and thrown into a jail to be put to death by a laser-beam firing squad, will you stand with fear?" I shout.

Cam jumps back and takes the position of shooting laser beams to the right and then to the left.

"Fear will not cross my mind nor enter my heart, Cap'n," Izzy says.

"Well," I say, closing the Mission Control notebook for another day, "then I suppose we're ready for anything."

As I place the notebook back on my desk, I look at the picture of Gram, returned to its position in the corner. She wasn't right about foster care stealing your dreams. And she wasn't right about me being all Mama and Izzy have left. They have each other. And I have them, too. And together with Cam, I know we can all make things happen. If we get more momentum on the ground, if we run as hard as we can and stick together, someday, we're going take right off and land in the nearby stars.

Author's Note

WHEN I WAS WRITING THIS BOOK and having it vetted, I was asked, "Why are you writing a book about mental illness if you don't suffer from mental illness yourself?" I would like to endeavor to answer that question here, because mental illness is something I have debated writing about for a long time.

My mother has worked in the mental health field her entire adult life. When I was little she worked at a recovery residence for those suffering from mental illness. I would go with her to work and spend time with the residents there. I remember liking the people quite a lot. To me, they had big imaginations. One said his mind was a thousand years old. Another was Joan of Arc reincarnated. Another had a collection of baby dolls to mother. Another could tell you every result of every Red Sox game ever played, from memory. To me, it was clear they had stories. It also became clear that they had people they loved and people they missed. They had times where they were happy and times when they were sad. They had interests and skills. Things they loved and things they hated. And just like everyone in the world, they had good days and bad days. When I went to school, classmates seemed to be wary (to say the least) of the people who lived at this recovery center. They would bring up unfounded rumors. This made me wonder, Why are my friends afraid of something that I know is just fine?

It occurred to me at a later age that perhaps the rumors and the wariness sprang from ignorance. Not in a malicious way, but in an unintentionally uninformed way. That is where the stigma of mental illness enters. What does *stigma* mean? Stigma is, by definition, a mark or stain of discredit. Think of it this way, if you only watched TV and read books about mental illness, would your view of mental illness differ from if you knew someone who suffered from a mental illness in real life? In our media, is mental illness shown in a certain way? Think of all the books and movies that you could read about GOING INSANE! The horror of the asylums? The Mad Genius. The characters on the verge: possessed or psychotic? Our culture is rife with grandiose and terrifying tales of losing one's mind. Stories that depict mental illness, more often than not, show it in a very scary negative, and often violent way. This all feeds a stigma of mental illness in our society. When I set out to write this book, I wanted to make sure that Mama didn't fall into that category, that she was realistic and whole.

As far as I see it, story immersion of any sort is an empathetic experience. In writing, in reading, in watching or playing, you have the chance to immerse yourself in another life. So while working on this story, I had the chance to understand Mama's backstory, her passions, her heartbreak, her goals. I had the chance to see how those might affect—be interpreted and misinterpreted—by those around her. I had the chance to work from the inside out and look at how similar Lucy and Mama were in their thinking, though different from each other in most aspects of their lives. They both have goals, have passions, have love for each other. They are not as different as they may seem at first blush. I hope that I have done the characters in this book justice and—even in a small way— made it easier for those who do not know people suffering from mental illness to recognize the humanity in us all.

While reading, you may have noticed that Lucy felt like she had to fix everything on her own. And at the same time, Mama felt alone in her loss of her mother and felt like she had to fix everything. Unfortunately, this isn't an abnormal feeling. But it isn't true! Did you know that 1 in 4 Americans will suffer from a mental illness in their lifetime? Luckily, there are some great resources that can help. I especially liked listening to the personal stories on each site.

National Alliance on Mental Illness (NAMI):
Personal stories about mental illness, online discussion groups, local NAMI resources and so much more:
http://www.nami.org/

Mentalhealth.gov:

Hope and recovery stories, support networks, as well as information on health insurance and services: www. mentalhealth.gov

All Kinds of Minds (TED Talks):

For personal perspectives on mental illness: http://www. ted.com/playlists/9/all_kinds_of_minds.html

OK2Talk Campaign:

PSA campaign to make mental health a conversation, call a hotline, find resources and stories: www.ok2talk.org

National Institute of Mental Health (NIMH):

For education, articles, research: http://www.nimh. nih.gov

American Psychiatric Association (APA):

For articles, research, and advocacy: www.psych.org

Acknowledgments

THERE ARE SO MANY PEOPLE WHO contributed to the writing of this book. First off, thank you to Ma for bringing me to Waterbury to see the art installation and hear the voices at the state hospital. Thank you also for reading the manuscript in earlier drafts and steering me in the right direction with the details. Thank you to Carolyn Dobbins. Your book *What a Life Can Be: One Therapist's Take on Schizo-Affective Disorder* inspired and informed me and having your insight was instrumental to the credibility of the manuscript. Thank you to my UN Critique Group: Barbara Crispin, Tamara Ellis Smith, Cindy Faughnan, Trinity Peacock Broyles, Jennifer Wolf Kam, Sarah Wones Tomp, Sharry Phelan Wright, Cynthia Vaughan Granberg, and Sherry Shahan for encouraging me in the very first pages. Thank you to the VCFA and EMLA communities for sharing your worlds with me near and far. Thank you to Jessica Dainty Johns and Ginger Johnson for the writing days. Your steadfast diligence always inspires and pushes me forward. As always, thank you to the team at EMLA, especially super agent Ammi-Joan Paquette, for being in my corner. Thank you to the team at Philomel, but especially to my amazing editor, Jill Santopolo. You always ask the right questions and know how to stick the ending. This book wouldn't be what it is without you.

As always, thank you to my friends and family for putting up with me and cheering me on while working on this manuscript. Special thanks to my sisters, Casey, Moie, and Ambs, who are always an inspiration. Thanks to Ma and Pa for being great people. Your love and example always inspires me. And last but never least, thanks to my love, Howie, who gets me. You're the best.